THE SCANDAL
BEHIND THE
ITALIAN'S
WEDDING

THE SCANDAL BEHIND THE ITALIAN'S WEDDING

MILLIE ADAMS

MILLS & BOON

First published in Great Britain 2020
by Mills & Boon, an imprint of HarperCollins*Publishers*
1 London Bridge Street, London, SE1 9GF

Large Print edition 2020

© 2020 Millie Adams

ISBN: 978-0-263-08921-9

This book is produced from independently certified FSC™ paper to ensure responsible forest management. For more information visit www.harpercollins.co.uk/green.

Printed and bound in Great Britain
by CPI Group (UK) Ltd, Croydon, CR0 4YY

For the book girls.
Keep dreaming.
Keep reading.

CHAPTER ONE

IT WAS RUMORED that Dante Fiori could condemn a man to any level of hell he chose with the mere lift of his brow.

Powerful. Ruthless. Determined.

Dante was not a man to be trifled with or tested. He'd raised himself up from the slums with the aid of his mentor, Robert King, but then not only had he gone on to exceed the man's expectations, he'd increased his fortune, as well.

Dante was a force in the world. A man all other men looked to—save his best friend, Maximus King, who found him overrated in the extreme and was the only person who had the nerve to say so. A man all women wanted to be with.

A king in whichever kingdom he chose to rule, whether he was a King by blood or not.

So it was shocking, then, when the world

turned on its axis right in the middle of the King family's grand living room.

Dante was in town, and he'd been invited over, as he often was, to join the family for their rather loud and raucous get-togethers. They were celebrating the launch of their oldest daughter Violet's new makeup line, in a live video being broadcast from a nearby San Diego beach, to millions of viewers on her various media platforms.

Robert was lounging in his oversize chair, his wife, Elizabeth, sitting on the arm. Maximus was sitting back on the couch, one leg flung out in front of him, phone in one hand, a scotch in the other.

There was one family member missing. Two, actually. Minerva King, the youngest daughter and constant irritant, and her baby.

Dante had difficulty accepting the existence of the newest, smallest member of the King clan.

Min was nothing like Maximus or Violet. Maximus was a brilliant PR mind. A handler to the most difficult clients in the world. He did everything with a smile that the untrained eye might not be able to see was shot through with steel.

Violet was stunning. Keen and ambitious, she'd transformed her beauty into a multi-million-dollar enterprise. She was the driving force and face of her brand.

Then there was Min.

A little brown mouse who scurried about the grounds, always trailing about the place with animals dripping from her arms and a skinned knee. Her cheeks were always red, her hair always in a state.

And she talked. Constantly. About nothing.

She'd gone abroad to study nearly one year ago, and when she'd returned, it had been with a baby who was barely a month old. While initially shocked, over the past four months her family had accepted the existence of the little girl easily enough. The Kings weren't old-fashioned.

The shock hadn't come from the fact their daughter had broken with tradition and had a child out of wedlock—presumably with a foreign stranger—but that it had been Minerva and not Violet.

Dante did not feel accepting of it at all. He felt a strange burning in his chest when he looked at Min with the baby. This untamable, wild thing now tied down to earth by a child. By motherhood. She should be...out climbing trees. No matter that she was twenty-one, he couldn't wrap his mind around the fact that she was a woman now.

A *mother*.

The other urge he had was to find the man who had done it to her and send him back to dust.

Send him straight down to the ninth level where he could sit next to Lucifer himself.

It infuriated him perhaps because Minerva always seemed so hapless. Running around like a windmill, and falling down, often undented. Though she had been badly dented once at an event of her father's, and he remembered it well.

Some boy she liked publicly humiliating her on the dance floor.

Robert King had nearly had a stroke, and his anger had only embarrassed Min all the more.

She'd been seventeen or so. Dante had danced with her because she'd needed a partner.

Don't let them see you cry.

He'd said it sternly. More than he'd meant, but it had done the trick.

The idea that someone had harmed her now enraged him all over again.

He wasn't in the habit of questioning himself. He simply acted when he felt action needed to occur. And perhaps that was the issue here. There was no action to be taken.

It didn't matter. Minerva didn't matter. Neither did her current situation.

All eyes were on Violet and would be for the next fifteen minutes while she unveiled her next series of products. And then it would be time for Dante to speak to Robert about the joining of the two companies again.

He had been trying to tell Robert it was the best thing for everyone. And, of course, some of it was that Dante felt entitled to King Industries as he had helped to build it. He had gone off and made his own fortune, but his ultimate goal was a merger between the two.

Of course, Robert had feelings about keeping it all in the family.

But Maximus had no interest at all. Maximus was a billionaire, and his business methods were unorthodox. He had no interest in manufacturing.

Violet was much the same, and while she used King Industries to help make her products, she developed them on her own, and used her father's business simply for the manufacturing end, containing development and distribution within her own brand.

Only Minerva remained to take over the family business, and he knew that Minerva would have no interest in such a thing.

She was not… Ambitious.

Minerva was not brave.

If she were here now, it would be as if she weren't. She would simply be sitting in a corner, clutching her baby and looking around.

Unless she began to chatter.

But typically, she was quiet as her father commanded during times such as these.

Violet's beautiful, perfectly made-up face appeared on the screen, and the whole family paid heed. Dante looked up, sparing the screen only a glance before looking back down at his own phone.

But then, a moment later it wasn't Violet's voice he heard.

"I know you're watching to hear about my sister's products, and not to hear family gossip. But, as her new makeup line is called Rumors, I thought that I would put some rumors about me to rest."

He looked up and saw his brown mouse.

There was Minerva, her dark hair hanging loose and unstyled past her shoulders, not straight, not curled, somewhere in between. She was holding the baby, gripped tightly against her body.

"There has been much discussion in regards to the paternity of my baby girl. I'm used to being the King that no one has any interest in. And yet, the interest surrounding Isabella's birth has been unprecedented for me. Well, it's time for the secret come out." Brilliant green eyes met the camera, Min's only stunning feature. And they were glowing now. "The father of my baby is Dante Fiori."

Whatever else was happening on the screen, not a single person in the family was watching now.

All eyes had turned to him.

He looked into his friend's eyes. And he saw only murder there.

She had done it. In a panic, she had done it, and Violet had been more than happy to allow her to step up and make the announcement because Violet loved nothing more than a spectacle.

Well, Min had promised her spectacle. She had delivered.

And now, in the limo, after the announcement was done, Violet had exploded.

"Dante?"

"Yes," Minerva said, lying through her teeth and feeling more and more terrified by the moment.

"Dante? Dante slept with you?"

She couldn't work out if Violet was shocked because Minerva was not the sort of woman Dante typically went for, or if Violet was angry that Dante had touched her, or if Violet was angry because she was... Well, maybe a little bit jealous.

Violet was the great beauty in the family, there was no questioning that. Minerva wasn't much at all. She never had been.

Until she had returned from a trip overseas with a baby. And then speculation about her had begun to swirl. She should have known there would be no avoiding rumors. She should have known that avoiding the press would be impossible. She should have known that every jerk with a smartphone would try to take her and Isabella's picture, and that those pictures would be posted everywhere, for anyone in the world to see. And that Carlo would see them. And he would suspect.

And once she had gotten the threatening text, she knew that she had to act.

She was in danger. Isabella was in danger.

She didn't believe that Katie's overdose had been purely accidental, and she never would. Carlo was the kind of man who had access to all sorts of things, and her friend had been terrified during those last days of her life. Because he had found them.

It had been so simple for a while, to stay under the radar in Europe. Minerva wasn't a particularly famous face, in spite of her connection to the King family, and outside the United States nobody ever gave her a second glance. If she had been with Violet, everyone would have recognized them.

But on her own, she was just a university student. The same with her friend and roommate.

But clearly, Carlo had figured out who she was, and where she was.

And worse, where Isabella was.

She had no choice but to tell this lie. To throw him off the scent.

Because this baby could not be Carlo's baby. Not if it was hers. Not if it was Dante's.

There was a reason the deception about Isabella had been so paramount when she had first come home. That she insisted the child was hers.

Everyone had believed it. And she had thought it would be enough. It was one reason she hadn't worried over much when photographs of herself and Isabella had begun circulating.

She had never slept with Carlo. Therefore, any child of hers could not be a child of his. And besides, she was used to her superpower. Invisibility.

A wren among a gaggle of peacocks, Minerva was simply accustomed to being forgotten. She didn't imagine for a moment that Carlo would remember her face. He had only seen her a handful of times during the time she'd spent studying in Rome. And he had been entirely focused on Katie.

But clearly, he had begun to piece things together.

And so...

And so.

She had promised her sister a show. She had delivered.

But she did *not* seem pleased.

"Dad is going to *kill him*," Violet said.

"Do you think so?" Her father had responded to her return with a baby in an extremely sanguine manner. As far as Robert King was concerned, as long as none of his children were crack addicts he had done fine enough.

She had asked him if it bothered him. That she had a child without a partner.

He'd said: "Why would I mind? You're not a teenager, and you have the money to take care of her. It's not like the house isn't big enough."

And that had been the end of it.

She couldn't imagine he would be angry simply because the baby was Dante's.

Dante, on the other hand…

She could only hope that he was somewhere far afield. On the East Coast. In his New York office. Perhaps he would be in Frankfurt or Milan.

Just so long as he wasn't…

The limo pulled up to the front of the King family mansion, and all of Minerva's hopes and dreams were dashed when she saw him standing there.

Her heart nearly lurched up her throat and out of her mouth.

She had forgotten.

How imposing he was. How large.

How utterly, devastatingly handsome.

Which was ridiculous, because she had seen him only a month earlier.

She could still remember the awkward, horrible dance at one of her father's parties. Her biggest crush ever had only agreed to be her date for a dare. To see the inside of the infamous King mansion and to report back to friends at school.

Dante had taken hold of her after Bradley had embarrassed her, and held her close, shielding her from curious eyes. He'd been so strong and solid, and all the anguish and shame inside her had caught fire and burned hot. It had been so embarrassing but she'd also been unable to pull away from him.

But he'd been pity dancing with her. He'd added to the confusion of…everything.

And compared to Bradley's bony shoulders, Dante's had felt so broad and solid.

It had all been weird.

Even with that she could forget.

But she didn't think that the impact of a man like Dante Fiori could live in its genuine state inside a woman, or anyone. You would die of it.

It became clear only in person.

He had always made her feel small. Rattled.

She had the tendency to run at the mouth whenever he was around. He made her stomach feel like it was quivering.

She disliked it intensely. And yet, she had always felt drawn to him like he was a magnet. She had always felt compelled to get a response out of him. To go to him. And she could no more understand any of those tendencies then she could understand quantum physics.

Which was to say: not at all.

"He is unhappy," Violet said softly.

"Well… He'll just have to deal with it."

Minerva lifted her chin, affecting a posture of determination she did not feel. Her brother appeared behind Dante, and behind him was her father.

Everybody *did* look remarkably unhappy.

Min was not accustomed to being the source of people's unhappiness. She was used to being ignored, and when she'd shown up with her parents' first grandchild, they'd been happy.

No one looked happy now.

The car stopped, and Dante didn't wait. He marched over to the car and jerked the door open.

And she found herself face-to-face with his stormy black gaze.

It was fathomless. As if she could look all the way down into the depths of his soul. Into the depths of hell itself.

She knew the things they said about him. That when her father had encountered him in Rome when he was a boy, Dante had been attempting to rob Robert King at gunpoint. That something about the boy had made Robert pause. That he had given him his watch, but also his card, and told him that if he wanted to change his life, rather than just live to commit another robbery, he should contact him.

And that shockingly, Dante had.

But that he had been a man who had committed a great many atrocities prior to his salvation and education that had been financed by Robert King.

She had never believed the stories.

Mostly because her father loved a story, and it was one he did not tell. Which forced her to believe that the truth of it must be less dramatic, and far less interesting.

Now she wondered, though.

Because she felt like she was staring down the very devil.

"We have a lot to discuss, don't you think?"

Dante took hold of her hand, and lifted her from the limo, depositing her gently onto her feet. She looked past his shoulder, at Maximus and her father.

"And when you're done speaking to her," Maximus said, "I think you and I need to have a talk."

"I'm sure this will give you time to rally the firing squad," Dante said, his tone dry.

He was still holding her hand.

She could recall, with perfect ease, another time Dante had touched her hand. Not the dance, but earlier.

She had been a girl. All of twelve, and she had fallen out of a tree in the backyard.

Dante had found her lying pitifully on the ground, pondering her fate, and he had been afraid that she had broken her neck. He had yelled as much at her as he had lifted her up. His touch, hot and strong, had started to quiver low in her body.

She hadn't liked it. She had pulled away from him, then bent down to wipe the blood from her knee. "I'm fine."

"You are a menace," he'd said back.

She could imagine the exchange happening just that way now.

"I have to get Isabella," she protested.

"Go," he said.

She did, stumbling as she went. With shaking fingers, she undid the seat belt and lifted her baby girl up from the seat.

The thing was, it didn't matter who'd given birth to Isabella.

Minerva was her mother.

She'd cared for her from the time she was born while Katie shrank away in increasing fear, self-medicating away the terror of the possibility of Carlo finding them.

Min was not brave by nature. But she'd known someone had to be brave for Isabella. And since Katie couldn't, it had to be her.

They walked past her brother, who was looking at Dante as though he wanted to flay him alive, and her father, who looked stoic. Into the house. Up the stairs.

Totally silent.

Minerva clung to Isabella, thinking of her in some ways as a shield. Surely not even Dante would yell at her while she was holding a baby.

He opened up the door to her father's study, and ushered her inside, slamming it behind them. "Explain this, Minerva, because you and I both know that I am not the father of your baby."

Well, she was disappointed on that score. Dante was clearly fine yelling around an infant.

She cupped the back of Isabella's downy little head. "Did you tell them?"

"No, I didn't tell them. You're going to have

to tell them, because if I tell them they're not going to believe me. In the hour it took you to get home from the press conference, I had to tell your brother about ten reasons he shouldn't kill me where I sat. And the leading one was that I might be the father of your child, and that you might need me in some capacity."

"I *do* need you," she said.

Silence settled between them as he waited for her to explain.

"I'm sorry," she said finally. "I panicked."

"Why did you panic? What is happening?"

"You were the only name I could think of. The only name that was big enough. I had to protect myself, Dante. I had to protect Isabella! And I thought seeing as you are so close with my family, it was believable enough that you and I…that we…"

"Yes, well. The problem is, *child*, that the idea I would touch you in that way is laughable in the extreme."

Minerva had never felt so small, or quite so dull.

Standing next to the brilliant Dante Fiori

made her feel as plain and inadequate as she was.

He was right. The idea that he would touch her was laughable, though it seemed as if Maximus and her father were more than willing to believe it. So why wouldn't the rest of the world?

She knew he'd only ever danced with her four years ago because he'd pitied her. Everyone knew it.

Still, she held her head high.

"Men are renowned for touching women that don't make sense. It is common knowledge that the secret sexual fantasies of men are *unknowable*." She leaned in and did her best to seem confident when she was very much not.

"Is it?" he asked. "Well, mine are fairly knowable. Often plastered on the front page of newspapers here and there. *You* are plainly not my fantasy."

She thought of all the women he'd been seen with over the years. Sleek, polished and curvy. Brunette, blonde, pale or brown, didn't seem to matter to him, but there was a so-phistication to the women he enjoyed.

Quite like her sister, and not at all like her.

"Well, that is good to know," she said.

"Why did you do it, Minerva?"

"I am sorry. I really didn't do it to cause you trouble. But I'm being threatened, and so is Isabella, and in order to protect us both I needed to come up with an alternative paternity story."

"An *alternative* paternity story?"

She winced. "Yes. Her father is after her."

He eyed her with great skepticism. "I didn't think you knew who her father was."

She didn't know whether to be shocked, offended or pleased that he thought her capable of having an anonymous interlude.

For heaven's sake, she'd only ever been kissed one time in her life. A regrettable evening out with Katie in Rome where she'd tried to enjoy the pulsing music in the club, but had instead felt overheated and on the verge of a seizure.

She'd danced with a man in a shiny shirt—and she even knew his name because she wouldn't even dance with a man without an introduction—and he'd kissed her on the dance floor. It had been wet and he'd tasted of liquor and she'd feigned a headache after and taken a cab back to the hostel they'd been staying in.

The idea of hooking up with someone, in a circumstance like that, made her want to peel her own skin off.

"Of course I know who he is. Unfortunately… The full implications of who he is did not become clear until later."

"What does that mean?"

She could tell him the truth now, but something stopped her. Maybe it was admitting Isabella wasn't her daughter, which always caught her in the chest and made her feel small. Like she'd stolen her and like what they had was potentially fragile, temporary and shaky.

Or maybe it was trust. Dante was a good man. Going off the fact he had rescued her from a fall, and helped her up when her knee was skinned, and bailed her out after her terrible humiliation in high school.

But to trust him with the truth was something she simply wasn't brave enough to do.

Her life, Isabella's life, was at risk, and she'd lied on livestream in front of the world.

Her bravery was tapped out.

"Her father is part of an organized crime family. Obviously something unknown to me at the time of her...you know. And he's after her. He's after *us*."

"Are you telling me that you're in actual danger?"

"Yes. And really, the only hope I have is convincing him that he isn't actually the father."

"And you think that will work?"

"It's the only choice I have. I need your protection."

He regarded her with dark, fathomless eyes, and yet again, she felt like he was peering at her as though she were a girl, and not a woman at all. A naughty child, in point of fact. Then something in his expression shifted.

It shamed her a little that this was so like when he'd come to her rescue at the party.

That she was manipulating his pity for her. Her own pathetic nature being what called to him, yet again.

But she would lay down any and all pride for Isabella and she'd do it willingly.

"If she were in fact my child, then we would be family."

"I… I suppose," she said.

"There will need to be photographs of us together, as I would not be a neglectful father."

"No indeed."

"Of course, you know that if Isabella were really my child there would be only one thing for us to do."

"Do I?"

"Yes." He began to pace, like a caged tiger trying to find a weak spot in his cage. And suddenly he stopped, and she had the terrible feeling that the tiger had found what he'd been looking for. "Yes. Of course, there is only one option."

"And that is?"

"You have to marry me."

CHAPTER TWO

TWO THINGS HAD become clear to Dante as he'd stared down into Min's green eyes.

The first was that if Minerva and Isabella were in real danger then he would have to protect them. There was no choice.

He could not uncover her lies, because no matter how convoluted it might be, his protection was perhaps the only thing standing between her and this man she claimed wanted to do her harm. Dante was not so foolish as to think he could simply involve law enforcement and make an issue like a man connected to a crime family go away.

But he had resources. Men at his disposal. And more important, he had money. If her plan didn't work, he had other methods of being able to protect them.

And then, there was the second thing that occurred to him. Which was that if he wanted a stake in Robert King's company, then marrying his daughter, and being the father of his granddaughter, was likely the best way to accomplish that.

Dante had always known he would marry. It was a given. He had no plans to love his wife, as indeed he had no plans to love, much less the ability. But he had always thought that he might want a son. Someone to carry on what he had started.

He was a man from nothing. Nothing had been given to him. And he had much that he could pass on to an heir.

So yes, he had often thought that he would marry. Why not Minerva? Why not when it would benefit them so?

No, he would never be attracted to the skinny, dull little hen, but it didn't matter. They already had a child between them, as far as the world was concerned. And genetics meant nothing to Dante. The man who had fathered him had gone off God knows where and hadn't given a damn about him. While his mother...

She had cared the best she could. But she

had been an old, tired whore—in a literal sense, not a euphemistic or insulting one—and in the end, the comfort of drugs was much more enticing than the grind of impoverished motherhood.

She had given up taking care of Dante when he was about eight years old. And she had given up living when he was ten.

He had been on his own ever since.

And while he was not sentimental, not really, on that score, he felt some measure of passion over the idea of protecting Isabella.

He did not need to become emotionally entangled in order to do this. It required legal paperwork and public trappings, and it was all the sort of thing he could engineer easily without needing to change diapers or rock her to sleep in private.

He also felt some grudging admiration for Minerva.

Minerva was protecting her child. She had come up with the solution that had seemed best to her in a moment of panic.

And he had the means to protect a child.

He would not leave Isabella exposed. Not as he had been.

After all, he had been dependent upon the good graces of a man who had not been his father. Robert King was, in many ways, the closest thing he had to a father.

No, genetics were not required to make a family. Genetics, however, had been required for him to gain access to Robert King's company. And now...well. Now he'd have a link there, as well.

"Marriage?" She recoiled. "You have to be kidding me."

"I'm not."

Where did she get off looking horrified by the prospect of marrying him? He was the one who would be saddled to this plain little creature from now until eternity. *He* was the one who ought to be concerned.

"Yes, Min, marriage."

"You're *old*," she said.

He barked a laugh. "And you're a child. But you wanted my protection, and I am willing to give it. But you have to give me something in return."

"Marriage."

"Yes."

"What are your motives? Because I know it isn't to gain access to my bed."

"Indeed it is not. But what I would like is for your father to consider merging his company and mine, and barring a family connection, he is not interested." Her green eyes were jewel-bright and full of rage.

"So you're willing to help me, but only as it benefits you in a business sense?"

"Please, Minerva," he responded. "I don't need this. Make no mistake. Had I needed a family connection I would have pursued it on my own terms long ago. With Violet. Not you."

Her cheeks flooded with color. "Oh, really?"

"She is much more in keeping with my image."

"Your image!"

"Though, to be perfectly frank, little one, I could have seduced you at any point over the years if I'd wanted to. I did not need your little scheme. Had I wanted to marry you, I'd have done so."

She looked a second away from howling. "You could not seduce me, Dante Fiori," she spat. "I don't even like you. I never have."

"Oh, is that why you used to follow me around like a puppy?"

He did not know why he felt the urge to prod at her, only that he did. She was the one who had walked them into this situation, and now she was going to put up a fight because he had found a way to make it tenable for him. Well. He would not have it.

This little sprite did not own him, and she was not in charge here.

If it weren't for the fact that he was not quite the monster that the press made him out to be, he could destroy her farce easily. All it would take was a simple paternity test.

"You are using me to clean up for your bad choices, Minerva. All the better for you if you'd been seduced by me. Because at least I would have offered marriage, and I would have posed you no threat."

"You are a threat," she said darkly.

"A threat to what?"

"Common human decency."

The door to the study opened, and Robert King filled the space. "I think we need to have a talk," he said.

"Whatever you have to say to Dante you can say in front of me," Minerva said.

"I don't think that's true, Min," her father responded.

"It is," she said stubbornly.

"Fine," Robert responded. He slammed the door behind him. "How dare you use my hospitality so poorly. She's a child compared to you."

"You weren't angry when I came home with the baby!" she protested. "But now you're mad?"

"Why rail at you for your decisions?" Robert asked. "You were out in the world on your own, and you did not consult me on your choices. You came home and presented them, and what was the point in holding a postmortem on it? I'm not angry at you. I'm angry at him."

"That doesn't make sense," Minerva shouted.

But Dante knew that it did. Because Robert knew exactly where Dante was from. Not only that, he was thirteen years Minerva's senior. A man who had seen more and done more than Minerva ever would.

She had been cloistered, sheltered by her family connections, and Robert had extended the same to him.

Robert had always counted on Dante to take care of Minerva.

Oh, yes, the fact that he was treating it as a betrayal made perfect sense to Dante.

And it spoke volumes about Minerva's actual inexperience and age that she did not.

"Just tell me that you never took advantage of her when she was younger," Robert said, his voice like iron. *"Tell me."*

"I would not," Dante said, keeping his voice even. "I swear to you, I would never abuse what you gave to me."

"And yet," Robert said, "here is the evidence that you have."

"I seduced *him*," Minerva proclaimed.

Both of them turned to look at her. Dante wanted to laugh. There she was, looking as she ever did, a university student in a sweater that was overlarge and a slouchy pair of jeans.

He couldn't imagine her seducing a trembling virgin. Let alone a man of his vast experience and particular appetites.

"It was the night of my going-away party. Before I went to study overseas." She gave her father a conspiratorial look and lowered her voice. "He was very drunk."

Madre de Dios...

Dante remembered that night well. He was not drunk, and had in fact been in the company of a lush heiress who was much more age-appropriate to him.

"I've *always* had a crush on him," she continued as the color rose in her face. "Yes. You see, I've always wanted him, and I thought that before I left I would get what I wanted. So I crept into his room and I... Well, I'm afraid I took advantage of him."

"Min," he bit out. "Stop helping."

"It's true! You were reduced. Your senses. I apologize for my predatory behavior. And I was ashamed. That's why I didn't... That's why when I found out I was pregnant I hid it."

"And why did you decide to announce it on TV today?" Robert asked.

"Well," Minerva said, clearly hunting around for an excuse.

And if Dante weren't so irritated he would be entertained watching her scrabble around for a reason why she'd chosen to reveal all today. And in public. She squinted. "I had been trying to talk to him. But he hasn't been returning my calls. I assumed because he was embarrassed."

"I was embarrassed?" Dante asked.

"Well, you were quite drunk," Minerva explained, like he was a child. "I don't know that you were up to your usual standards."

He could strangle her. Cheerfully. If she weren't holding a baby he might.

Her father, for his part, looked badly like he wanted to exit the conversation, and at least on that score he could give Minerva some points. She had successfully turned an uncomfortable situation into a horrific one, and Robert no longer looked angry so much as he looked utterly and completely appalled.

"You will, of course, do the right thing," Robert said, directing that at Dante.

"Of course," Dante returned.

"What's the right thing?" Minerva asked.

"Obviously he's going to marry you," Robert said.

"In fact, I informed her of this only a moment before you came in," Dante said. "She's being stubborn. She has no concept of the consequences of her actions."

"Well, then it will be up to you to ensure she does."

"Dad," Minerva said, her tone scolding, "stop playing the part of tyrant. It doesn't suit you."

"It does, however, suit me, *cara mia*," Dante said.

She shot him a fearsome look.

He would never have ascribed a word like *fearsome* to Minerva before. She had always seemed timid to him. But standing there, cradling her baby as she was, her posture defiant and defensive, he found that *fierce* and *fearsome* were words that described her extremely well.

As irritating as he found the situation he was in, he could only admire it.

That she was a woman willing to do whatever it took to protect her child.

Along with that came the discomforting thought of her being touched by a man who was involved in organized crime.

What had happened? Had the man seduced Minerva? Had she seduced him? Was it a piece of truth buried in the outrageous story she had made up about taking advantage of Dante while he was drunk?

Minerva was twenty-one, but he couldn't imagine that she had a very long or intense history with men. For as long as he'd known her she'd been unattached, and she had never seemed overly interested in that kind of thing.

He was basing that off her total lack of efforts when it came to making herself up. Her sister was a makeup mogul. If Min wanted to improve herself she could have easily done it.

But then, the fact that she had come back with a child, the fact that she had claimed for all the world that he was the child's father, and the fact that he had never guessed she would do any of those things made him acutely aware of the fact that he didn't actually know her that well at all.

"Your mother will want to speak with you," her father said.

"I imagine Maximus will want to speak with me," Dante said.

Robert gave him a long look. "Yes. I imagine. Though as you are marrying her..." He appraised him slowly. "You do know, I suppose, that this will put King Industries in your hands."

"It had occurred to me." There was no point pretending it hadn't. Robert knew him too well.

"Had the timing been different, I would've suspected you of nefarious behavior, but you never inquired about the child, or made any effort to see if it was yours."

"It didn't occur to me the child could be mine," Dante said. "And no, I didn't plot this."

"No," Robert agreed. "A plot of yours would've been much neater."

Dante grinned ruefully. "Well, at least we both agree on that."

"I will leave you for the time being. But Dante, the wedding must be planned sooner rather than later. Now that it is revealed, you will move to make an honest woman of her. I do not want speculation to go on. Our official statement will be that fearing you wouldn't be receptive, Minerva kept it from you, and the moment you found out..."

"It's not a story," Dante said. "It's the truth."

Then Robert turned and walked out of the study, leaving the two of them alone again.

"You're a fool, Minerva. Did you not think that me marrying you was inevitable?"

"It never occurred to me that my father would force the issue. He was so... Lackadaisical about me being a single mother. About me returning with a stranger's baby."

"Yes, because he cannot force a man he's never met to act with honor and integrity. But he would expect it for me. Surely you must have known..."

"I didn't think about it," she snapped. "When Carlo texted me, I panicked. I did the only thing I could think to do. I jumped in front of the cameras. I don't regret it. Even now."

"Good. I'm glad to hear that you have committed to lying in the bed you've made."

"How long do you suppose we'll have to stay married? It seems to me that we should be able to have Carlo dealt with in a timely fashion, and even if we don't… Well, if we can keep up the facade for a long enough amount of time, then surely he'll fade into the background eventually."

He regarded her closely. "*Cara*, I'm Catholic. Divorce is out of the question."

CHAPTER THREE

MINERVA HAD BEEN stewing on his sudden devoutness to his latent Catholicism for two weeks.

He couldn't be serious. He absolutely *couldn't* be serious.

Their marriage would have to have a term limit. She couldn't stay married to him *forever*. She wouldn't *need* to. And the idea of being shackled to Dante for her entire life…

It made her feel like her skin was too small.

She was the last woman on earth whom he wanted to marry, and surely at some point in her life Minerva deserved to be something other than last.

She didn't regret taking Isabella on. She could have allowed the police to take her into custody when she'd come home with Isabella and found out the news about Katie.

She hadn't had to claim that Isabella was hers.

She could have come home with her and found her another home here in the United States, where she would maybe even be safer from Carlo.

But she… She felt like Isabella was her child.

She'd cared for her during Katie's depression.

Her stewing was productive ultimately. Because by the time the evening of their engagement party rolled around, she had realized the perfect solution.

He was *Catholic.*

Which meant that while divorce was complicated, there were ways around those complications. They would only need an annulment. Provided, of course, that the marriage wasn't consummated. And she was well aware that that would cause some slight issues with their ruse, but by the time they separated they wouldn't need it anyway. And neither she nor Dante was in any danger of temptation to consummate.

She was feeling borderline triumphant by the time she met with her sister to get her hair, makeup and wardrobe done for the event that she didn't even want.

But her family was under the impression that this was a real marriage, and not only was it a big deal because she was getting married, it was a big deal because Dante was getting married. The fact that they were getting married to each other was making it a whole King family spectacle.

"You need gold," Violet said authoritatively. "Gold eye shadow, gold bronzer, a gold dress."

"I'm going to look like an award," Minerva pointed out.

She was feeling out of sorts because she did not have Isabella with her. Her mother had Isabella for the time being, and then for the party itself she would be up in her room with a nanny attending.

"Well, that is exactly how you should look,"

Violet said. "Like a prize that Dante has won, right?"

She looked at her sister's sullen face. "Except, you think that *I've* won the award," Minerva said. "The award being Dante."

Violet's eyes locked with Minerva's. "I don't really. It's fine. I had a slight crush on him for a while, but I'm over it."

"I'm sorry," Minerva said. "I really didn't know."

"Mom said that you had a crush on him for years."

"*Honestly*, the rumor mill in this family."

"She said you had a crush on him for all your life." Minerva felt doubly guilty, because not only was she marrying the man that her sister had feelings for, her own feelings were a fabrication.

"Yes," Minerva said, her throat going dry. "It's why I always followed him around."

He was the one who had brought that up.

That was not why she'd followed him around. She had felt compelled to interact with him. To be near him. Like a person might stare at a big cat through the bars of a zoo cage.

He was wild and compelling, and it had never failed to call to something inside her. Though, she didn't know what to call that thing.

Maybe it was because nothing in Minerva was wild or compelling at all.

She was bookish, and she was a tomboy, and she was ever injuring herself while running around outside imagining she was various literary characters that she found between the pages of her books.

She'd been called a dreamer more than once. Someone who didn't connect well with the harshness of reality.

And so there was something about the darkness simmering beneath the surface of Dante's skin that she had always found wickedly interesting.

Like he was a dragon in folklore.

And that was down to her rather dreamy nature, as well.

It had nothing to do with him. And it certainly had nothing to do with feelings of any kind.

If she had any sort of feelings for him, it was that sharp, tangled-up gratitude over his helping mitigate the shame of her being rejected in front of an audience and then, of course, the way he was helping her now.

"It doesn't matter," Violet said. "I haven't really fancied him for ages. But he is handsome. You have to admit."

Minerva felt her face getting hot, and she wasn't sure why.

Violet shook her head and rolled her eyes. "Of course you already know. You've seen him naked."

The temperature in her face increased. She had not seen Dante naked. And she would not.

But surely her sister knew all about these things. Violet was so lovely and smooth. She did so well at parties, mingling with important, high-powered people everywhere she went. Her ability to harness her image and control a brand was renowned.

She imagined her sister was much more

sophisticated when it came to men than Minerva was.

Then, the average sixteen-year-old was slightly more sophisticated when it came to men.

Of course, no one could *ever* know that.

"Let's get you fixed up," Violet said.

And true to her word, Violet did fix Minerva up. Quite well, in point of fact.

And she had been right about the gold. It took her mousy brown hair and made it something else. It surprised Minerva that she had left her hair mostly unstyled. Letting it fall in waves down her back, though it seemed much glossier after her sister had sprayed something on it, and the gold leaf headband that she had woven into her hair made it all look very intentional, rather than that Minerva's hair sat somewhere between curled and straight, and she didn't know what to do with it.

The dress she was wearing made the most of her slight curves, and the plunging neckline looked elegant, and not trashy. A gift, Minerva supposed, of having a very small chest. If her more voluptuous sister had worn the dress, she would've looked stunning, but the effect would have been different.

"I love it," Minerva said, but her stomach felt hollowed out, and her body felt unsteady. She lifted her hand to touch her hair and her sister caught it, examining her bare fingers.

"I do hope that Dante is planning on giving you a ring," Violet said.

"Oh," Minerva responded. "I hadn't even thought of it."

"You do want to marry him, don't you?"

"I need to," Minerva said. "Desperately."

"Good," Violet said.

Well, it hadn't been a lie, she did need to marry him. It just wasn't because of her emotions or anything like that.

Her sister had been kind to her, and rather than putting her in heels had chosen a pair of sparkling, pointed-toe flats that were actually quite pretty. They were also very comfortable. And made Minerva feel like less of a gangly, awkward deer than she might have if she had been up on stilts.

She left her sister's bedroom, nearly ready

to go down to the party, when she ran into her mom coming up the stairs.

"I was just coming to fetch you," she said.

Elizabeth King was a stunningly beautiful woman, more along the lines of Violet and Maximus than Minerva.

They all looked a lot alike and there was no question of the fact that they were siblings, but there was something about the way her parents' features had rearranged themselves on both Violet and Maximus to be an even more pleasing configuration. And somehow, on Minerva it had always seemed wrong.

Her nose was similar to her mother's, but it was longer, more like her father's.

Her mother had a full upper lip, slightly more so than her lower, which gave her the brilliant look of a rather exquisite doll.

Minerva's was yet more imbalanced, her cheeks somehow looking round, rather than sculpted, in spite of the fact that Minerva didn't have an ounce of extra fat on her body, nor curves to speak of.

What was commanding height on Maximus was gangly on her.

Her mother's hair could be called a brilliant toffee, while Minerva's was more mouse-ish.

"I'm here," Minerva said.

"You look lovely," her mom said. "Are you ready?"

"Yes," Minerva said, suddenly feeling horrendously insecure. "Don't I look ready?"

"Of course you do," Elizabeth responded. "That isn't what I meant. I meant… You want this, don't you, Minerva? Because I will tell your father to call the whole thing off if you don't. I know that he got angry and he insisted that Dante do the right thing, but if you don't love Dante then this isn't the right thing."

Bless her mother, who only wanted her happiness, but of course this wasn't for Minerva. It wasn't about Minerva.

It was all right, she was used to that. Nothing in her life had ever truly been about her.

Every member of her family was a brilliant gem that shone brightly in their own right. Her mother was a former model and beauty queen. Violet modeled herself, and additionally was a business tycoon. Maximus had taken his share of their father's fortune and multiplied it exponentially. His face was famous, his business acumen renowned.

And her father...

California King had been the headline of business pages for years, along with the requisite mattress jokes. But Robert King was not a joke. He was one of the most highly successful manufacturers the world over. Managing to be both savvy and profitable, while maintaining a strict standard of treatment for workers.

Only Minerva was *nothing*.

And she had been content to be, in many ways. *Privileged* to be.

Because there had been no pressure for her to go out and make something of herself in order to survive.

Her survival had always been a given. Because no King would be tossed out onto the streets if they failed to make a living for themselves.

Her survival had always been a given until Isabella. Until Carlo.

The one good thing about all of this was

that at the very least she had discovered that when things were difficult she did possess the mettle to get through it.

"You don't have anything to worry about," she said to her mom. "I know what I'm doing."

Really, for the first time in her life she felt like she knew what she was doing. At least with a grander and broader purpose than simply trying to stay unnoticed.

And everything would be fine in the end. Because this would buy her time, it would keep her safe, and then she and Dante could be free of each other.

Her mother escorted her down the stairs, to the exquisitely decorated backyard.

Their home and the large courtyard overlooked the beach and the ocean. The family had private access, and the whole stretch of sand belonged to them.

There was a bonfire already going there, and the sun had set, casting an orange glow that faded to purple in the sky, silhouetting the palm trees that lined the shore.

So many people had come, and she didn't know any of them.

She had friends from school, but most of them were out of the country still.

And, of course, poor Katie was gone.

Oddly, the fact that the place was littered with strangers, and faces that she only knew because she had seen them plastered on television screens and newspapers, hit home the point that she was doing the right thing.

That what she did she did for Isabella, and it was important.

Certainly of more significance than the rest of her life.

But it was the sight of Dante that unraveled something inside of her.

He was wearing a white shirt, the sleeves rolled up, and a pair of dark slacks that somehow made her very aware of the fact that his thighs were powerful.

Which she thought had to be the oddest observation in the history of observations.

"Glad you could join us, *cara mia*," he said.

"Of course you knew that Violet wouldn't allow me to show up until at least an hour after the party had started," she stated.

"Of course," he responded. "That seems an incredibly Violet perspective on things."

"One has to make an entrance. One cannot do that if they arrive early."

"Well, I had no idea I've been doing entrances wrong this entire time."

She studied him, his sculpted jaw, his imposing height and his broad shoulders. "Honestly, Dante, I imagine whatever time you arrive you create a spectacle."

"Thank you," he said, inclining his dark head.

"That was *not* a compliment," she said.

"I took it as one. Anyway, you must look happier to see me, Minerva," he said. "As you *are* madly in love with me. So madly in love with me that you decided to seduce me in an inebriated state, taking terrible advantage of me and my agency."

She rolled her eyes at his ridiculousness. "I had to say *something*. Otherwise my father was going to skin you alive."

"I believe the offer of marriage was sufficient. Though I appreciate your efforts to protect me." He said the last part so drily she could tell that he didn't mean it at all.

"Well, you're of no use to me if you're dead. You can't protect me then."

"I don't know. If Carlo believed that your dad killed me because I had fathered your child..."

"Well, I don't want you dead," she said. "Not at the moment. Though—" she held a finger up "—I have arrived on a solution to your issue of divorce."

He narrowed dark eyes. "Have you?"

"Yes," she said brightly. "Obviously we'll get an annulment."

His dark eyes flicked up and down. "An annulment?"

"Yes! Because we won't consummate."

The look he treated her to could only be described as pitying. "Minerva, on what planet would anyone believe that?"

"You said yourself that you are not... attracted to women like me. I'm not offended by that. I'm not attracted to men like you." She patted his forearm, then removed her hand quickly when she found him disturbingly hot and firm. She cleared her throat. "Your tastes are public. So, no one will be surprised."

"Except the public, and your family for that matter, think that we had a child together."

"A fluke. And we will claim that there was no spark left once we married. And at that point Carlo won't be an issue. So it will be a mere blip in the headlines."

"Minerva, it would be a blip in the headlines if it were only you. But sadly, I am included in this, and I am more than a blip in any headline."

Minerva sighed heavily. His ego was such a massive yoke over his shoulders it was a miracle they were so straight and broad. They should be sagging beneath the weight.

Sadly, nothing on the man sagged.

"It *will* work," she insisted.

"So you think that your father will blithely allow me to leave you?"

"If we explain."

"Explain?"

"Once..." She looked around. "Once Carlo is no longer an issue we can explain everything to my family. And at that point he'll be so grateful he will likely allow you to continue on with your efforts in the company."

He looked at her as though she were a child, his expression nearly pitying. "It is not something we need to concern ourselves with."

"We simply need to concern ourselves with *not* consummating."

He looked at her for a long moment. "I will try to control myself."

The arid reply left her feeling scraped raw, and she trailed after him at the party rather angrily thereafter.

But of course she couldn't *look* angry.

She had to look pleasant.

It was very strange, acting the part of accessory to someone. She had never done it. And here she was, keeping position next to him, moving as he did, trying to mirror his body language, and facial expressions, so that they seemed as if they were in one accord, whether they were not.

By the time they had made their rounds, Minerva was famished, which was only adding to her mood.

Then Dante swept her aside, taking both of them out of the glow of the string of lights that went overhead.

"It's time to put on a show, *cara*."

"Show?"

"Yes," he said. "I have a ring for you."

"Oh," she replied.

"Look surprised," he instructed as he grabbed her hand and dragged her back beneath the lights.

"Of course I'll look surprised," she whispered. "I *am* surprised."

"Try to look *happy* too," he said.

She had no time to respond to that before he had turned toward their guests and, somehow, by his very motion commanded the attention of the crowd.

Minerva stretched her lips into a wide smile that she had a feeling fell flat around the corners.

"As this has come together very quickly, there is one aspect of our courtship that I have neglected. We have done a great many things out of order, Minerva and I."

This elicited light laughter from the crowd.

Of course, in the rather sophisticated culture of the rich and famous in Southern California, having a baby before marriage—or without marriage at all—was not considered out of order.

But no doubt the chuckles were in deference to the presumably more conservative culture Dante came from.

"And in all the activity I have neglected to give Minerva her ring. I will do so now."

He pulled a ring box out of his pocket, and he did not drop down to one knee. "I've made the request already, I think," he said, opening the box and presenting it to her. It was huge. A statement piece if ever there was one, and she herself was so very not a statement piece that it seemed shocking, and nearly vulgar.

But he didn't ask her, and instead was sliding the monumental rock onto her finger.

As if...

As if something so magnificent, something so glorious, should be there. On her thin, fine-boned hand that was not manicured or elegant or anything of the sort.

She recalled her school friends had once likened her hands to *claws*.

And there was Dante Fiori's ring.

On one of her *claws*.

Min swallowed hard, and when she looked up at him, he was gazing at her with sharp intent. It pierced her, made her feel like she couldn't breathe. And before she could do anything, say anything or decide how she might react, he was moving in toward her.

All that sharp intensity was focused on her, and somehow she could feel it gathering in her stomach, nearly painful.

He was so close they were breathing the same air.

And then, his mouth was on hers.

His mouth.

This, *she knew*, was not kissing.

It couldn't be.

She had been kissed before by that stranger in the club, and that hadn't been kissing either. Because it had been unpleasant and cold, and it made her want to run, rather than embrace the man giving it.

But this…

It was not romantic.

It was not gauzy and sweet, wrapped in warm summer breezes and crashing waves. Blooming flowers and other grand literary euphemisms.

It made something in her stomach twist hard. Made her feel like some creature was biting down on her windpipe. The feel of his lips against hers was so *real*. So very physical. They were warm, and firm, and as he took command of all things, he took command of her mouth.

Shifting her slightly so that she was fitted more firmly against him.

All in all, the kiss was not terribly long, and it was not terribly intimate, but when it was done she felt like she had been hollowed out, her hands shaking, her whole body shaking.

And he looked… As unreadable as ever. Utterly infuriating, that man. He was like a block of obsidian that could not and would not be disturbed, not by anything. Least of all by her.

He had just handed her a ring, and then he

had pressed his mouth to hers and tilted her entire world on its axis.

And there he was. Like a guardian of the underworld, completely unbothered by the whole thing.

The audacity of the man.

He had just kissed her. And he hadn't had permission. She would badger him about it, but she had the distinct impression that he wouldn't care.

"Shall we go mingle, *cara mia*?"

He whispered that question in her ear, and he made it look as though there was an intimacy between them that there just wasn't.

That is the entire point of all of this. Keep it together.

But she was having difficulty keeping it together. Because he was very large and hard beside her, and because she had always liked the idea of creating an effect in him. When she had followed him about and pestered him when she was a girl, part of it was that she had enjoyed seeing if she could get a reaction.

But right now it was clear that he would always have the upper hand. She would never,

ever be the one to get a superior reaction out of him. He would always be the one to create havoc in her.

Because that was what it was, wasn't it? Her chasing after him. He was affecting her. She had always imagined herself leading the charge in those interactions. But it wasn't true.

It was him. It always had been.

Even in this, even in her scheme, he had somehow managed to take charge.

It was demoralizing. Dispiriting.

In front of all these people, downright humiliating.

She felt red and sore and exposed somehow, and she couldn't pinpoint why.

"Smile," he whispered, bending down, his lips nearly touching her ear, a shiver winding down her spine.

And so she did.

She had to remember that this was for Isabella. It wasn't for her.

And her own discomfort had nothing to do with it.

For Isabella, she could do this. For Isabella she could do anything.

It wouldn't be forever.

She stared at his patrician profile. No. Whatever he said it would not be forever.

Dante Fiori might be used to running a business. He might be used to commanding women, manipulating them with his good looks and power. And maybe in the past he had had an effect on her behavior, as well.

But she knew now. Was unbearably conscious of it.

Minerva King might be the least famous of her family. The least successful. And the least powerful.

But she was also stronger than anyone knew.

And in the end, that strength was going to carry her through.

CHAPTER FOUR

IT WAS HIS wedding day. His secretary had informed him firmly on Friday that this was to be the happiest day of his life.

He'd done his best not to laugh at her. Because she was sincere and just because he didn't possess the ability to see the world in such a pure fashion didn't mean he had to destroy the illusions of others.

Dante had never been under the impression that this would be a joyous day for him. Rather, he had always known that it would be a calculated move that benefited him in some way.

But this… This was not what he'd envisioned.

They had put the wedding together very quickly, and Min had been lying low in the meantime, rarely leaving her parents' house, at his express command.

Though she had told him with great umbrage that she didn't need him to command a single thing because she was completely happy to hide until they had made things legal between them.

Security. That was all. Just added layers of security.

Dante was not a man who believed in taking unnecessary chances.

He was standing in the back room of a cathedral sanctuary with his future father-in-law and his future brother-in-law standing on either side of him.

He had not imagined that Robert and Maximus would be in that position. Had it been another scenario, he would have imagined they were offering support. As it was, he had a feeling they were making sure he didn't run away.

It was all a bit close and familial for his taste.

He would always appreciate what Robert King had done for him, and if he had a friend, Maximus King was the best one he possessed.

But the way that they were with each other, the ease that the family had with one another, had always made his skin itch.

He was not familiar with these sorts of dynamics. Not privy to the way families typically acted with one another. He didn't understand. He hadn't grown up with it.

If he had siblings, then he didn't know any of them. His father had never been part of his life, and his mother had died early, and even before then she hadn't exactly been the model of maternal care.

He wasn't angry about those things. It was simply life.

Life, in his estimation, was not fair, from conception.

You could be born into a family like the Kings, or you could be born into the streets of Rome as he had been.

You could have a father like Robert King, or a father like Isabella's who was threatening the life of her mother and trying to drag her into a criminal underworld that was no place for anyone, let alone a child.

These things were accidents of fate and there was no point railing against them.

There was only making decisions about what you would do with the things you were given.

Dante believed that firmly.

He had made the most of what he'd been given. He had been given a hand up, and he had taken hold of it.

But that didn't mean that he felt completely comfortable with his situation, or his position.

In some ways, he would have imagined that Maximus would be with him on his wedding day in this capacity. He just hadn't imagined he would also be related to the bride. And that was where the connections became uncomfortable.

"If you hurt my sister," Maximus said, smiling and clapping his large hand on Dante's shoulder, "I'll kill you myself."

There weren't many men who stood at eye level with Dante, but Maximus was one of them. With ice-blue eyes and blond hair, he was a Viking counterpart to Dante's fallen angel.

He would never have thought of something so fanciful, but when they had gone out together in the past, women had made such comments.

Which gave Maximus's threat a lot more weight. After all, Maximus had seen up close Dante's appetite for beautiful women, and he imagined that his friend's believing that such an appetite had spilled over onto his younger sister was something that was never going to sit easy with him.

In fact, Dante imagined the only reason that he wasn't dead was that he had fathered a child—supposedly—with Minerva.

Had they simply been caught in a compromising position, he imagined that Maximus would have simply dispatched him on the spot.

"I believe it," Dante said, because he knew that was better than any empty promises that Maximus would have discarded.

And he *did* believe it.

They were friends, it was true, but they were not blood.

The King family was connected by blood.

Dante had no such connections. And it was fine by him.

"You have always been like a son to me," Robert said.

And Dante knew that the old man *thought* he meant it. But Maximus had never had to worry about whether or not he could have access to sharing his father's company.

Dante wasn't bitter about that. It was just a difference. One that he was ever aware of, even if Robert was not.

"I suppose we had better get things started," Dante said.

"Nothing will start on time," Robert responded, looking at his watch. "I believe Violet is in charge of hair and makeup?"

"Yes," Dante said. "I imagine she's also in charge of entrances."

"What?" Robert asked.

"Never mind."

They filed in from the back, and all of them

took their places. Robert made his way back to where the bride was.

It hit Dante then that whatever differences between himself and Maximus, Robert was seeing to the double duty of being father of the groom and bride.

Had Dante been capable of feeling warmth over such a gesture, he would have, he was sure.

The crowd that filled the sanctuary, Dante knew, was not enthralled by any love story between himself and Minerva. No, they were hoping to gain the attention of either himself, Maximus, Robert or Violet.

It hit him that no one would be here for Minerva.

It was a strange thing to be bothered by. He had rarely given consideration to Minerva beyond cursory. But Minerva didn't possess anything that anyone might want.

He was under no illusions that anyone was here because they cared about Robert or Maximus or Violet.

They cared about what any of the aforementioned people might be able to do for them.

He wondered if that was how Minerva had been vulnerable to a man like Isabella's father. If she had been left vulnerable because of her position in the family.

As he had been thinking earlier, life was very much what you fashioned from what you were given. Minerva could have created anything.

As it was, she had created a baby with a dangerous man. And that had been her decision.

But not Isabella's.

And if he was being magnanimous in any way, then it was on her behalf, because he knew what it was to be a child hamstrung by his parents' poor decisions.

And yes, there was the matter of getting to have possession of King. That did matter to him.

What he had not expected was for Minerva to look quite so lovely last night. And for the kiss to send a jolt of electricity through his body.

The very strange thing was that Minerva's reaction was…unreadable.

She had been angry with him at some point during the evening.

She had not gone pliant, she had not melted against him, she had not responded at all.

Quite the opposite, she had been stiff. She had been still against his mouth, behaving like a woman who didn't know what to do.

He had done his best to seize control of it, to change the tenor of things, but she had not allowed it.

And he could not for the life of him figure out if it had been inexperience or disgust that caused her to react in such a way.

Mostly because he had never kissed a woman who found him *disgusting*.

But then, he had never kissed a woman for show.

What made him most irritated was the fact that he was not disgusted by her.

Minerva wasn't *beautiful*.

There was a prettiness to her. It was simply that she was also a bit plain, and he preferred something a bit gaudier. He had been raised, after all, with a prostitute for a mother. For the years when she'd been well, she'd been

all hair, perfume and jewels, and it had been
the same with her friends who had passed
through their run-down apartment. His concept of beauty was a bit more bedecked.

She was also young. The younger sister of
his friends, and because of that she'd been
firmly off-limits from moment one.

The fact that she had the power to effect a
response was irritating in the extreme.

The bridal party began to come down the
aisle, though it was a simple bridal party. Violet walking arm in arm with Maximus, who
came to stand next to Dante. He flashed his
friend a smile.

"I will kill you," he whispered, never breaking that smile. "I did mean it."

Dante said nothing. But a grin tugged at the
corner of his mouth as he turned to face the
doorway of the cathedral.

And suddenly there she was.

Her hair had been twisted and gathered up
into a complicated style that was loose and
sparkling, thanks to jewelry of some kind
that had been woven in.

The dress itself was simple, soft, flowing

fabric that seemed only barely there. It rested over her curves like a fine mist. With each step she took, the long billowing lilac fabric swirled around her.

Something had been applied to her cheeks that made them glow in the candlelight, her lips, pale and shimmering.

She had been made up, but it was still very much her. Even more so than it had been the night of their engagement party. And somehow it was as if it had uncovered the essential beauty that Minerva possessed. A beauty he had never seen before.

She was ethereal. Like a creature of the earth transformed into one of the sky.

A treasure that had been hiding only to be brought out and polished now.

When she looked up at him, her green eyes shone bright, and he could see that it was her. And suddenly, the Minerva that he knew every day blended with this one, and he knew that he would never be able to unsee the beauty, even if she were to revert back to the way she'd been before.

When they joined hands, a sly smile crossed

her face. Anyone watching would be forgiven for mistaking it for intimacy.

"I'm glad you decided to follow through," she whispered.

"I would not abandon you," he said, offended by the assessment he might.

"No," she said, frowning. "Of course you wouldn't."

The priest began his solemn intonations and there was something about the way Minerva held herself, about the strange expression on her face that caused a response in the vicinity of Dante's heart.

He had to wonder if for Minerva, this was somewhat conflicting.

He should not feel sorry for her at all, given the fact that she was the one who had gotten them into this position in the first place.

She was the one who caused this, and if she didn't like the end result, that was her problem.

But he couldn't overlook the fact that she was softer than he was. That for her, marriage was never intended to be a cynical meeting of people who wanted to firm up business deals.

No, for Minerva it was never supposed to be that at all.

That she had gotten herself into this mess, and the fact that he had twisted it to suit him as well, wasn't something he was going to waste time feeling guilty about. He didn't waste time feeling guilty in general. It was a fruitless exercise. Just like wishing that a pauper had been born a prince.

Or that a street urchin from Rome had been born a King.

It did nothing to solve one's problems.

For him the vows were easy. But she hesitated over each promise she made, possibly because she was afraid of what would happen when she didn't keep them.

It hadn't been nice of him to make fun of her about not being able to divorce.

He had done a great many things the church wouldn't approve of. He was hardly going to start worrying over much about his eternal soul now.

At the end he could go to confession, take his penance and spend the last bit of his life atoning.

He was far too busy to atone now.

But, the question of the permanence of the marriage was a tricky one considering that it would impact his portion of ownership with King Corporation. He had a feeling that Robert King would take an even dimmer view of Dante divorcing his daughter than he did to Dante marrying her in the first place.

That was a considerable issue.

Though, she did have a point. If when it was all said and done, they were able to explain everything, then Dante would possibly be considered a hero when she told the tale. Something he wouldn't have asked for, but a possibility.

It wasn't as if he wanted to stay married to Minerva forever.

When it was finished, it was time for them to kiss again, and she shrunk away from him.

One thing was certain: he could not stay married to a woman who shrunk away from his touch.

He wrapped his arms around her and she gasped slightly.

He didn't give her time to react. Because if

he did, he feared that she was going to cause difficulty.

He crashed his lips down onto hers. Swallowing her gasp and parting her lips with his tongue.

He didn't know why, but he felt compelled to affect her. Perhaps because she had affected him, and it didn't seem right that she'd had nothing but a negative response to him. An unreadable response.

A nonresponse.

He had a kick in his gut the moment he related that desire to instigate a response from her with the way that she had followed him around when she was a young girl.

The way that she had always been trying to gain a response from him.

It was petty. And it was childish.

But he allowed his tongue to delve between her lips anyway.

And she tasted… Like sunshine. Spring. Something that was indefinably Minerva.

Still, she was frozen beneath him. Her hands clutched at his shoulders, but they were motionless. Not impassioned in any way.

And when they parted, it was like yet another veil had been ripped from his eyes.

He could no longer see a girl.

But a woman.

That hint of fearsomeness that he had seen when she had defended Isabella shone through those green eyes now.

Not a hen. Not a mouse.

A tigress defending her cub.

He had misjudged her.

And for a man like Dante Fiori, this was a terrible sin. He was never a man to misjudge or underestimate an enemy, an adversary or a potential partner.

But he had misjudged Minerva.

He had looked at her, and he had seen all that she had shown the world, which was only a facet of what she was.

He wondered what Isabella's father had seen of her.

He couldn't help it. Was she a tigress for him?

He despised the other man.

They were presented to the guests, but he

was not conscious of what was being said, or what was happening.

There was a ringing in his ears.

They charged down the aisle and into the waiting room where he assumed that Minerva had been before.

She went over to her purse, and diaper bag, and began to root around inside, pulling out her phone.

"Eager to check your social media?" he asked drily.

"No," she said. "I'm worried. Because our wedding is today, and I'm concerned that…" She went pale. "He texted me."

She handed the phone to Dante.

I feel that I should come to the reception so that I can have a look at the child and see if she is indeed mine.

"Well, he's not getting near you, or Isabella," Dante said. "And at this point, I think we should inform the police that you have been receiving unwanted attention from a stalker. Nothing more."

"Do you think?"

"He's organized crime, and he's not from here. But if he does set foot in the country, he will face legal recourse from the law here. That's important. We must make sure that we put barriers in his way. And in the meantime, you and I are going on our honeymoon early."

"We are?"

"Yes. We are. Somewhere where he won't find us."

"Where is that? Because he found me, and he found her."

"No offense, *cara*, but your family is quite conspicuous, and you are known to live here. Plus, he clearly has your mobile number."

"I didn't give it to him," she said. "I got a new phone the moment I set foot onto American soil again. I changed my number."

Dante swore. "Well, it's no matter. I own an island, but it is not in my name, and it's hidden by a shell company. No one knows about it, and he won't know where to look. There will be no way for him to discover our whereabouts, and I will be using private investigators to make sure I find ways to remove him as a danger to your safety."

Her eyes went round. "In what way will you remove him?"

Dante waved a hand. "That is not your concern."

"Dante… I don't want you to do anything illegal."

He chuckled, low and dark. "That ship has sailed, I'm afraid. Or do you not know how I met your father?"

Her shoulders narrowed. "I thought that was just… A story."

"It is a story that has been greatly watered down."

He saw himself then, a boy of fourteen, holding a handgun extended toward an older man, pressing it to his forehead.

His hands were shaking. He was sweating.

One of his mother's boyfriends had told him that if you were going to do this kind of thing, you couldn't flinch. You couldn't shake. And you certainly couldn't sweat.

Above all else you had to be willing to pull the trigger.

And as Dante looked into the calm, kind

face of the man that he was about to rob, he knew that he could not pull the trigger.

"Lower the gun, son," the man said in soft, clumsy Italian.

It was the kindness that immobilized Dante, for he had never known anyone to look at him with anything other than resentment, disgust or pity.

Until Robert King.

"You really held my father up at gunpoint?"

"I did," he said. "Believe me, I have no concern for what might happen to a mafioso. Men like him… Well, they bring ruin everywhere they go. They most particularly have brought ruin to my country, my streets. To women like my mother. They are part of a system that operates on fear and oppression. He is doing it to you in this personal capacity, but I guarantee you he has done it to many in a broader sense. I will not have it. I will not." He reached out and touched her face, and he suddenly meant those words more than he had ever meant anything in his life. "Nothing bad will happen to you or to Isabella. I swear it."

He took her hand, and led her out of the vestibule, and they nearly ran into Elizabeth, who was cradling Isabella, and Robert.

"There has been a change of plans," Dante said. "It seems that Isabella has picked up a stalker from her time overseas. She is being threatened."

"By who?" Robert asked.

"A man called Carlo Falcone. He's from a crime family in Rome. Whatever he says, don't listen to him. He's insane, and he will use anything he can to try to manipulate you and the situation. We must notify the police that he intends to show up at the reception."

Robert's lip curled up into a sneer. "I'm more than able to handle him by myself."

"Can you handle the retribution that will come if you dispatch him? It isn't the law I worry about, but the rest of the family."

That seemed to calm some of Robert's readiness for a shootout. "I don't want anyone in my family targeted by this man."

"No. So we're going to call for police presence at the reception, but I also want you to make sure that it gets out that Minerva and I have left. That we are not there. Have Violet post it to one of her social media accounts. I believe that he's tracking our movements this way. And also, if she would be so kind as to indicate we've gone on a honeymoon in Italy, that would be brilliant."

"But you won't be," Robert said.

"No. He will not be able to find us where we are going. I will be able to keep her and Isabella safe. You can trust me."

"I do," Robert said. "And that is not a statement I made lightly, Dante, and it is not a statement I would make to most men."

"You saved my life," Dante said. "With all that I am I will protect hers."

Robert nodded, and he took Minerva's hand, then he used one arm to scoop Isabella from Elizabeth's arms. He had never held the child before. He was surprised by the way that she felt. Warm, and like a feather.

A small little thing he could have cradled in the crook of his forearm.

"I will keep them both safe."

CHAPTER FIVE

MINERVA'S HEAD WAS spinning and she couldn't breathe. Didn't breathe in fact until Dante's private jet had lifted into the air. Only then did she believe that they might be safe.

Isabella was laid in a plush bassinet, and Minerva had no idea how Dante had managed to acquire it so quickly.

And in the time she spent wondering about that she found time to worry about photographs from the wedding. It was stupid.

But the headlines after their engagement party had been…

They hadn't been outright cruel, but they had included a photograph of her from four years ago.

Seventeen, with her face streaked by tears, and him so much taller and broader and outlandishly beautiful than she could ever hope to be.

She imagined that the implication of the photo was he'd been involved with her even when she'd been scandalously young, but looking at it she knew no one would ever take that seriously.

He was Dante Fiori. She was... Minerva the Mouse.

The girl who was worth a date only so her class could get a look at her house. And she'd heard later he'd wanted to get a look up her sister's dress, as well.

Violet had laughed herself hoarse after hearing that and then had gotten a deadly look in her eye. And Minerva had known if she'd ever seen Bradley after that Violet would unman him with the sharp end of her tweezers.

But that was the thing.

Violet was the hero in that story. The object of beauty and the one so above the idiocy she could laugh and make threats.

Dante was the hero in the story.

Willing to dance with her in spite of the fact she was gangly and unattractive and sad.

She was the object of pity.

And she feared when her wedding photos were splashed across the media it would be the same story.

Sad, pitiable Minerva snags a man due to a faulty condom.

Just thinking about *Dante* and *condoms* made her get hot to the roots of her hair.

"There will be supplies for her already on the island, as well," he said casually as he poured himself a drink and settled back into the plush leather sofa.

Minerva curled more deeply into the chair she was seated on, leaning over Isabella and adjusting her blanket unnecessarily. "How?"

"There are people that work for the shell company. They will be gone by the time we get there. None of them will ever know who gave the instructions. Who actually owns the house. They won't see us."

"Why do you have something like this?"

"I bought it quite a while ago as a precaution. Because one never knows when one might need to escape."

"Dante, you're not involved in anything illegal *now*, are you?"

"No," he said. "But when a man comes from a background such as mine he learns to be paranoid."

"I suppose. And I never did learn to be paranoid enough. Not until now."

Everything in her felt jumbled up.

She would love to think more about the kiss that he had given her at the altar. One that had turned so...intimate. But she hadn't had time to think about it or parse the way that it had made her feel, not in the face of the threatening text that she had received from Carlo so soon after.

"It is only a small island," he said. "The only building on it is my home, and the rest is unspoiled white sand and jungle. I think you'll like it."

"At this point, I like anywhere I'll feel safe."

For the moment, they felt united.

For the moment.

Dante busied himself with work during the journey, and Minerva slept when Isabella did, and woke when she was fitful. She marked the hours in feedings and diaper changings.

Until finally, the plane began to descend.

There was a small runway on the island, clearly.

"Your pilot knows where we are," she said.

Dante acknowledged this with a nod of his head. "I do trust him."

"*How much* do you trust him?" she pressed.

He lifted a dark brow. "Enough to allow him to fly me fifty thousand feet over the ocean?"

"Yes, but in that case his fate is tied to yours."

"Oh, believe me, Minerva, his fate will always be tied to mine. Because should anyone betray us—and in this case, the only option would be him as he is the only person on earth who knows we are here—his fate would be in a precarious position indeed."

"You're filled with death threats of late."

"Well, as is your life. Therefore, I find the situation merits more of them than I would typically be meting out."

Minerva pondered this as they got their things together and disembarked. She suddenly found him to be something of a stranger.

She had always known that he was hard, but she had also felt safe goading him. Now he had kissed her, and that made him feel unpredictable. And wholly different from what she had imagined he was.

Then there was his willingness to threaten someone's personal safety.

He did so with ease and without compunction. And it made her wonder what kind of man he was on a day-to-day basis.

She knew whom he was when he was interacting with her family, but she was beginning to think that wasn't the measure of him.

And given that he had actually robbed her father at gunpoint, she did wonder if Robert and Maximus had a better idea of who he was than she did.

Or Violet. Or Elizabeth.

She wondered if the women in the family were entirely ignorant of that side of him.

"You're thinking so hard I can see smoke coming out of your ears, Min," he said.

She tapped her chin. "I'm just thinking about your ruthlessness."

He lifted a shoulder. "People often do."

"Well, I didn't know that. You always seemed like somewhat of a stern older brother to me." She wrinkled her nose. "Stern. Not dangerous."

"Ah," he said. "An easy mistake to make, I suppose. Though, I don't think anyone else in the world has ever made it."

"Well, they don't know you like I do." She frowned. "Like I *did*."

They got off the plane and there was a car parked just there, waiting for them. It was fitted with a base for Isabella's car seat, and as soon as she was safely secured they were on their way.

The landscape was beautiful, and desolate as he had said. Dense forestation on one side, and brilliant white sand on the other. And there, built into the craggy hillside overlooking the sea, was an intensely modern, modular home, white squares to match the sand with glass all around.

"Home," he said. "For a while yet."

"It's very wild," she said.

He chuckled. "Wild?"

"Do you know what it reminds me of?

Swiss Family Robinson. More the film from the 1960s than the book, I suppose. But it's a very modern house sort of up in the trees in the jungle."

He nodded slowly. "I thought of that, as well."

She turned to look at him, feeling surprised. "Did you?"

"Yes. I quite liked that movie when I was young."

"Did you?"

"For a while I went to a free community day care center, and they had a few old films on VHS. *Swiss Family Robinson* was one of them. I always thought that would be a good life. Off on a remote island where no one could reach you. Where you didn't have to answer to anyone. And you could build whatever you wanted for yourself. Make whatever you desired. Resources from the land. Provided you weren't attacked by pirates, of course."

"I thought the same thing," she said. "But then, I also thought that I wanted to live on a farm on Prince Edward Island. And that I might want to live in Atlanta in a grand mansion." She sighed. "I've been so many places because of books. My college travels were supposed to be… They were supposed to be my big adventure where I could be the heroine instead of simply reading about heroines."

"And you brought back an enemy."

"I did," she said mutely. "I wanted adventure, but not quite like this."

"Well, you can have an adventure here. I promise you it will be safe."

Something about that promise settled heavy and hot over her skin, and she tried to ignore it. It was very disconcerting, the way his words had the power to affect her. They shouldn't. Things should be the same between them. Their mouths touching a couple of times shouldn't have profoundly shifted the balance between them any more than vows that had no honesty behind them.

"You've gotten very quiet again," he said.

"I should think you would like me to be quiet."

"I find it unsettling. Because it's not normal."

"I've never been accused of being normal, Dante. You of all people should know that."

Their eyes met for a moment, and she had the vague sense he could see something inside her she couldn't even see clearly herself.

"What possible attraction did a man like this have to you?" When he asked, the question was so rough and fierce it caught her off guard.

"What do you mean?"

"You don't seem like the kind of woman to be taken in easily, Min."

She sniffed loudly. "Who says it was easy?"

His expression tightened, even as he kept his gaze on the road. "He didn't force himself on you."

"No!" The denial came swift and fierce. She knew enough about Katie's story, and about what had attracted her to Carlo, that she could easily repeat it to Dante, but she found that she couldn't. She didn't want to talk about being seduced, not when she hadn't been. Nor would she take a trauma on herself that she hadn't experienced. So she thought it best just to change the subject. Deflect as best she could.

"It is impossible for me to say what the attraction to a man like him is." She placed each word carefully, as if it were a footstep in a minefield. "Once you know everything about his character, whatever might have been charming is lost. He's not a good man."

That much was true.

"And he is dangerous," she said, thinking of Katie again.

They drove up the house, and Minerva—who was used to a certain amount of grandeur—was utterly enthralled. Her family's opulence was like a mix of Tuscany and California. Ornate and lavish.

This was incredibly sleek and spare, but each detail was perfect. Everything about it looked solid, like the best version of itself.

It was—she thought—exquisitely Dante.

He was that sort of man. Not a spare ounce of body fat on him, muscular, honed. His suits cut to tailored perfection, sleek, dangerous lines. Nothing overshadowed him.

Rather it became a part of him. Absorbed into his orbit.

This house was no different.

He moved to the back seat of the car and retrieved Isabella's car seat, his movements as casual as if he had been doing it for the past three months.

"You're very good at that," she said.

"Thank you," he returned, and she couldn't tell if he was genuinely thanking her, or if he was making fun of her. She could never tell with him.

He made quick work of showing her the rooms about the place, and when he showed her to the beautifully appointed nursery she nearly collapsed.

It was an oasis. And Isabella would be safe.

Her daughter would be safe.

Whether Isabella had come from her body or not was irrelevant.

Carlo was her father, and he had blood ties to her, and it didn't mean that he cared. It meant nothing.

What mattered was love.

Isabella had given Minerva a sense of purpose she'd never experienced before. And yes, it had come with extreme exhaustion, uncertainty and a niggling feeling that she might be doing something wrong.

But mostly it was…purpose that she hadn't found before.

She'd left home to study in Rome because at home she'd always felt lost. She hadn't had a clear sense of what she wanted to study and she'd switched classes around at an alarming rate. History. Art. Art history. Business— which she'd quit immediately because it had depressed her since she had felt she would have to compete with Violet of Maximus to make it relevant.

But with Isabella she felt focused. She felt… fulfilled.

She gave Isabella a bottle, changed her diaper, and yet again, the little girl was ready to nap. Minerva took the opportunity to explore the rest of the house. Her bedroom was beautiful. Stark white walls, a white marble floor with the plush marble throw over it. The bedding was also white and soft, with large windows overlooking the sea. And she found that when pushed, they slid open, and were actually doors that gave way and led to a path outside. As far as she could tell that path led to the beach, and she had every intention of exploring it later.

For now, she needed a bath.

She slipped into the en suite and found a large tub that was also white, and looked like a freestanding bowl. It appealed to the romance in her spirit, and she began to fill it as she went back into the bedroom and began to rummage around for clothes.

It was then she realized that none of these were her own.

But of course they weren't.

Dante had procured a wardrobe for her. As she looked at the pieces, she couldn't imagine which woman he had been dressing when he had selected them.

Of course, Dante hadn't had anything to do with it.

But for a moment it was... Interesting. To entertain the idea that he looked at her and thought that she was the sort of woman who should wander around a place like this in a brief crop top, flowing pants and a sheer caftan. That she was the sort of woman who should wear many dresses in various bright colors and... A white bikini.

She hated wearing swimsuits, and she definitely didn't gravitate toward bikinis. Not when her sister often wore them in her signature purple, showing off her brilliant curves.

Minerva's curves were so slight she doubted she could even roll a penny down the slope of her breast.

She imagined herself in the swimsuit. If it got wet it might be somewhat see-through. She wondered what Dante would think of that.

The idea sent a sip of something forbidden through her body and she immediately turned away from it. She went back into the bathroom with the crop top, pants and caftan and stripped her clothes off, settling herself into the warm water. It was only there that she allowed herself to reflect on everything that had happened. The kiss...

She was submerged in warm water, and yet

she felt her nipples pebble when she replayed it in her mind.

No. She wasn't going to think of it. It was shocking. She should be angry at him, because he had kissed her in a way that no one would expect a man to do in a church.

Then she began replaying what he'd said about *Swiss Family Robinson*.

And that had an even deeper effect on her. Something that turned deep inside her and made her feel something in her chest.

She liked that even less.

The kiss was safer.

She got out of the tub hastily, wrapping herself in a towel and exiting into the bedroom. It was then she realized that Isabella was crying. Panic slammed against her, and she began moving around frantically looking for her clothing, but before she could, the bedroom door swung open and Dante appeared, cradling her in his arms.

Min just stood there, clutching the towel to her chest. "I was on my way," she said.

"I don't know what to do with the baby," he said, his tone accusing. "Take her."

She wasn't thinking clearly, and she reached out, taking Isabella into her arms, in spite of the fact that she was only barely wrapped in a towel. "I should've gotten dressed first," she said.

Dante paused, and looked at her, his dark eyes seeming to slowly register the scene in front of him.

"Neither thing is my problem. Handle it."

And with that he turned and walked out of the room, and she wondered where the caring man had gone who had told her about *Swiss Family Robinson*. Even the man who had issued death threats to the one who had indicated he might cause her harm was better than this one.

She didn't know why he was angry with her.

It was like he wasn't capable of holding a baby for a moment.

She sighed heavily and went over to the diaper bag in the corner of the room, hunting around for a pacifier. She popped one in Isabella's mouth, then took a blanket and spread it out as best she could with one free hand before setting her on the floor.

"I'm just going to get dressed," she said, keeping one eye on her the entire time. After that she saw her safely soothed, but she found that she could not soothe herself.

She was going to be stuck here with Dante for the foreseeable future. And she truly didn't know how she was going to survive.

She might be physically safe with him, but she didn't know what was happening inside her.

Didn't know what was happening inside him.

And like it or not, something about the vows that they had spoken had affected her. Had changed something in her.

What was a person to do when she found herself angrily married to her older brother's best friend and stranded on his private island?

You know what one of your heroines would do...

Minerva blinked, and pushed that thought aside.

It didn't matter what one of her heroines would do.

No matter what her dreams had been, she wasn't one of them. She never had been. And she never could be.

CHAPTER SIX

ALREADY THINGS WERE not going according to Dante's plan. And Dante had very little experience of things not going according to his plans. He was not a man who often had to deal with defiance, whether it came from another person, or life. Not a man who had been put in a position where another human being might come into his sphere and create disorder.

Chaos.

His life had been utter and complete chaos when he was a child. From the time he was born until he had been swept off the streets, half-feral, and put into a private school by Robert King.

Dante had been in possession of some concerns about Robert. Mostly, he had been convinced that a man who offered such things to a boy must have nefarious intent for him.

Dante had done a lot of thinking about whether or not he cared.

Because the streets had visited vast amounts of atrocities onto him. And when you were lean, and hungry, you tended to have a very flexible idea of what you might be willing to do for your next meal.

With that in mind, he had decided to take Robert's deal, and he had come to the conclusion that depending on what the man might ask of him, he would either comply and take the education, take the money for the time being, or he would follow through with what he had originally intended to do. Robert had given the gun back, after all.

All of those thoughts seemed so wildly removed from who he was now, and the kind of life he lived.

But it all came back when the baby had been wailing wildly, and he hadn't known what to do.

And then, he had gone looking for Minerva, only to find her standing there in a towel.

Her shoulders were enticing.

Her hair had been up, falling damply around

her face, and he had found it disconcerting in the extreme. And resentment had burned in his chest. For what he and Minerva both new was that Isabella was not his child.

And if she cried, she was not his responsibility. The responsibility was Minerva's.

And he would also like to speak to her about her responsibility when it came to not being an enticement.

Of course, he had no desire to admit to her that she was an enticement.

He ate dinner, and found himself at loose ends.

There was little work to be done, simply because he was not a man who was ever behind.

He took on work. More than he could handle, many would say, but he always managed to get it finished. And he was constantly being lectured on the fact that he should find a way to have more leisure time.

But for what?

He could never figure it out.

He went out when he felt like it. Oftentimes, there were business reasons to go out, connections to be made when he did. And then, if he managed to meet a woman in whose company he wished to spend the night, it was a pleasant diversion. But he didn't need more recreation time for that.

Often, words like that were spoken by those who didn't know what it meant to be hungry.

Who had never once had to entertain the idea that it might be preferable to endure the physical abuse of an older man in order to feed oneself.

No, in Dante's world, work and money were king.

It was a wall that he was building between himself and what he had come from so high and so thick that nothing would ever be able to cross it.

Safety.

He suddenly heard a soft voice, and the sound of a baby, and he turned and saw Minerva, wearing pants and a top that showed her stomach, coming down the stairs. "I'm starving," she said. "What's for dinner?"

"I ate," he said.

The look of thunderous fury that crossed her delicate features would have been amusing if it hadn't been quite so dark. "You ate? Without me?"

"I was not under the impression that we were required to eat in tandem."

"But what am I supposed to do?" she asked in a fury. "I would have thought that you would eat with me. *On our wedding night.*"

He cast her a flat stare. "Minerva," he said. "Don't tell me you were hoping for a more traditional wedding night."

Her mouth dropped open, then she shut it again. "Of course not. We mustn't consummate. Remember? Your Catholicism."

He huffed a laugh. "Thank you, for your dedicated concern to my Catholicism, but I promise you I have not forgotten it."

"Well."

"I wear it like a hair shirt every day."

"Fine," she said, her eyes green like beetles, and just as mean.

"Let's find you some food," he said. "I wouldn't want to get on the wrong end of you when you're hungry."

She followed him into the kitchen, and he opened up the fridge. He already knew that there was an elaborate charcuterie board in there, and some meals to be reheated. That was one of the issues with having staff off-site.

He did know how to cook for himself, but his skills were a bit crude, owing to the time in his life when he had to provide for himself.

Spaghetti with tomato sauce was all well and good for an eighteen-year-old going to university, but he had moved past that.

"You can start with cheese," he said, taking the platter and setting it out on the white marble countertop.

Minerva, clutching Isabella to her chest like she was a tiny shield, went over to the board and began picking at the offerings. She picked up a date, bit into it and closed her eyes, an obscene moan escaping her lips.

He gritted his teeth and turned away from that. "Fish or steak?"

"Steak," Minerva said. "Always steak. I haven't the use for fish."

"Well. I suppose that means you'll be consuming all the steak during our stay."

"I could give you a bite," she said.

"Oh, don't flatter me by offering me your castoffs, Minerva."

He took one of the meals out and began to heat the steak and vegetables in a pan for her.

She sat there, holding the baby with one arm and eating cheese with another.

"This really is very nice," she said.

"Oh, now your anger has subsided?"

"I don't know very many people who can stay angry while eating cheese," she said.

"You seem like someone who could," he said.

"I find that very flattering."

He had the distinct impression that she meant it.

He finished heating the food and set it out in front of her. He noted she was very comfortable being served.

She looked around. "Can you hold her?"

Several thoughts went through his mind all at once, careening around like a runaway train.

And he wondered for the first time—not just since this started, but in years—if he had miscalculated. He had assumed he could make a delineation between the public and private. Not have to handle anything to do with the child in private.

Clearly, Min thought different.

He had no experience with babies. He wanted no experience with babies. And, also, there was no way that he, Dante Fiori, could allow himself to be defeated by an infant.

Practicality dictated that Minerva needed both hands to eat. And that meant that he should hold the child while she did so.

"Give her to me," he said.

"You might want to work on your tone," she said, rising up from her seat and bringing Isabella over to him, depositing her into his arms. Then, she went and sat back down in front of her plate. The child was so light. She was barely a weight in his arms, and yet she was warm. She leaned against him, so trusting. So very... Fragile.

Minerva was busy eating, and he was pondering this. The baby's fragility.

How could adults leave small things such as this to fend for themselves? How could they ever put them in danger?

"I'll kill him," Dante said, his hand resting on the back of her downy head. "I will kill him for what he's put you through."

"Well, that's not something I expected," Minerva said, looking up from her plate.

"It is true, though. It is wrong, what he's done to you. And her. But mostly her."

"Well, thank you very much."

"We are adults, Minerva, and we must answer for our actions. A child like her has done nothing except be born into a broken world. She is helpless. She is dependent on the people around her to make decisions for her survival, her safety."

"I know," Minerva said. "And that's why I was willing to do whatever it took to keep her safe."

He nodded. "Of course. You would understand that."

"I do understand it. There was nothing to be done. I had to... Whatever the cost, Dante, I had to make sure that she would be protected."

Minerva ate in silence for a while, and then he shifted his hold on Isabella, who promptly made a sound like a very juicy hiccup and cast up her accounts on his shirt.

"Oh!" Minerva jumped up from her seat. "I'm sorry."

She reached out and grabbed hold of Isabella. And he looked down at his damp shirt. He gripped the hem and tugged it over his head. "I'll leave this for the staff when they come pick up the laundry."

"Staff?"

But her eyes were not on his face. Rather, they were resting in the center of his chest.

"Yes," he said. "We will make sure that we are not about when they come, but we will need to have supplies brought here, laundry dealt with, food replenished."

"Yes," she said, her eyes darting up, down and back and forth, but never going higher than his shoulders.

"Minerva," he said. "My eyes are up here."

And then she did look stunned. Her cheeks turning red.

Minerva was not unaffected by him. She was just very, very good at playing games.

He was shocked by this realization. But,

now that he had his shirt off, he seemed to have reduced her mouthiness by 20 percent or so.

"I know where your eyes are," she snapped. "I believe your shirts are upstairs, if you want to find one."

"I'm perfectly comfortable. Aren't you comfortable?"

"I'm not," she said, growing edgy and pink. "But that's because it's a little bit warm in here. And… I might walk down to the beach."

He arched a brow. "Might you?"

"I might."

He wouldn't have imagined that a woman— a grown woman with a child—could be made so uncomfortable at the sight of him without a shirt.

He knew that women found his looks impacting. It was something he'd enjoyed the effects of for the past twenty years. But he was used to purring, coquettish glances. Touching. Flirting. Not…fear.

"There's cake," he said.

Min tilted her head. "At the beach?"

"Here," he clarified. "Chocolate cake, if

you would like to stay for some. However, if you're indisposed..."

She sat, holding Isabella. "I will accept cake."

He chuckled, and went over to the other side of the kitchen, procuring a slice of cake and setting it on a plate.

He liked this reversal of fortune.

Because it had been bothering him that Minerva had had an effect on him, and now the tables had turned.

For a brief moment he saw his own actions, his own satisfaction, clearly.

He was delighting in some kind of sensual victory over Maximus's little sister. A woman who had been—until a few days ago—as a child to him.

But hell, they were going to be stuck here in this place for God knew how long. He supposed he had to take his victories where he could get them. He held the plate out to her, and with great effort, she looked up at his eyes.

CHAPTER SEVEN

SHE DIDN'T KNOW what was happening to her. She felt warm and flushed all over and she couldn't seem to do anything but stare at his chest.

She was trying to remember if she had ever seen Dante without a shirt before. She must have. At least when she was younger, and they went to the beach.

She was around shirtless men all the time. She lived in California. They had beachfront property.

She didn't know why this felt different, why it made her insides shiver, and why she felt overheated.

It had been strange to watch him hold Isabella, the way his powerful hands gripped her delicate body.

It made her so unbearably conscious of

his strength, and the control that he utilized in unleashing it. And now he was offering her cake.

And the image he made, shirtless and extending that decadent treat to her, his muscles shifting and bunching...

He had hair on his body. Not enough to conceal his muscles, but just enough to make her unbearably aware of his testosterone.

And that prickling in her skin was back. That racing in her heart, that unbearable, unsettling feeling that made her feel as if she had to do something. Anything. To get his attention. To get him to notice her.

And with a sudden horror, she realized what that feeling was.

And it was a feeling she had for a very long time. For Dante.

No. No. *No.* She wouldn't acknowledge it. She couldn't. She could not... Would not...

She had never.

And suddenly, she realized the little lie that she had told her father, her mother, her sister, might not have been such a lie after all.

Had she had feelings for Dante all this time?

That something in her simply refused to make them into the shape of what they truly were?

It was as if in that glorious chest of his she could see clearly. The most absurd thought she ever had in her life, but it was true.

Years of following after him, trying to climb trees in his sphere so that he might say something about her daring, talking and talking and talking at him even though he was so patently disinterested.

But she had never allowed herself to call it what it was, because he was far too old, far too beautiful, and if he was going to choose a woman from her family…

It would have been Violet.

It never would have been her.

Ever.

But maybe that was the real reason why the kiss in the club in Rome had felt so disappointing.

Because the man wasn't Dante.

And maybe that was why she had shut down completely the two times Dante had kissed her.

Because it wasn't real.

Because it was all a farce that she had set up, and if she really did feel this way, if the burning intensity of that bright something in her chest really did mean that she... That she had a crush on him, then perhaps using his name, using him as a solution, the fact that he was the father of Isabella, as a solution to her problem was...

The very idea made her squirm. Surely her subconscious hadn't done that.

But then, her subconscious was apparently a straight-up hussy for Dante, and she had kept her actual conscious from acknowledging that somehow.

And now, shirtless and with cake, she couldn't ignore it. Couldn't deny it.

Couldn't help but identify the sharp, reckless heat that had cut through her seventeen-year-old body the moment he'd taken her up into his arms to shield her from censure, to shield her from the world, had been...

Desire.

She snatched the cake from his hand and then looked down at it resolutely.

"Something wrong, Minerva?"

"Nothing is wrong," she said.

He approached her, and tilted her face up. "Nothing is wrong?"

He had touched her before. He had touched her many times, and this time it burned. Because this time she knew. Knew that that little prickling sensation he left all over her skin when his fingers made contact with her wouldn't happen with any man. Knew that it wasn't static electricity or something else that she could easily dismiss.

It was Dante.

But more than that, it was her feelings for him.

"I'm fine," she repeated.

But he was far too close to her.

"Good to know."

And then he moved away from her, and she realized, with stunning humiliation, that he was playing with her.

That he had known that she had been powerless in the face—or rather, the chest—of his magnetism.

She gritted her teeth and dug into the cake with ferocity. "I am fine. And I don't need you to eat dinner with me. After all, you ate already. You clearly didn't want to share a meal with me, so why hang around pretending? Go wash your shirt."

But he didn't obey. Rather, he stood there, watching her eat cake. And she refused to get up. Refused to let him win. So she ate every last bite, and then cleaned up each remaining crumb. Then defiantly rose, carrying Isabella in one arm, and the plate in the other hand, and deposited it in the sink before going back up the stairs. "I think I will get Isabella and me set up to have a date on the beach tomorrow. I know that you're very busy and have lots of work to see to. But it's fine. We will be just fine without you."

She was grateful that her hands didn't start shaking until she got back to the bedroom and closed the door firmly behind her.

Because she didn't want him to see just what he did to her.

It was beyond a cruel joke.

Because as Dante had said more than once, she was not the kind of woman who would ever turn the head of a man like him.

She was much happier when her brain had understood that, and buried her feelings for him, sparing her from any disappointment.

Now she just felt deflated and frightened and uncertain of how she was going to get through the next chunk of time.

CHAPTER EIGHT

THERE WAS A crackling fire burning beneath his skin, and he found it unconscionable.

True to her word, Minerva had been scarce the entire day.

When he peeked into the nursery, he saw that a great many of Isabella's items were gone, and he thought that it might be true that she had tramped off to the beach intent on staying there for the day.

Which meant that he would simply stay in the house and work. As she had said.

Dante had never had difficulty burying himself in work. No, quite the contrary, he had always found it to be a great solace. Another brick in the wall. But today he was restless, and today he found he would rather be outdoors.

Not a thought he often had, considering there had been a time in his life when he had been forced to be outdoors twenty-four hours a day, for lack of home.

Not that he didn't enjoy the beach on occasion, but he had been rather fond of temperature control since his first experience of it.

Before he could think much about it, he had stripped his T-shirt and jeans off, and gone on the hunt for swim shorts. Once he had acquired those, he took hold of a light T-shirt and put it on before making his way down the path that led to the private beach.

The sight of Minerva and Isabella did something strange to his chest. It tangled things up in there. And he didn't like it.

Minerva was wearing a white bikini, and he had never seen so much of her skin. She also had on a wide-brimmed sunhat, and she and Isabella were beneath a cabana, staying out of the sun.

Minerva's skin was that golden California-girl tone, courtesy of a lifetime spent at the beach. She had no makeup on today, her hair a riotous tangle beneath the hat, and he was sure that she had been out in the waves at some point. Her curves were slight, but they were delectable, her midsection slim but strong, muscles visible in her stomach.

Her arms were the same, slim but toned, as were her legs.

Her breasts were small, but round and high. His hands would eclipse them completely.

The thought sent a slug of desire straight through him.

What a strange moment. Standing there, looking at her as though she were…an object of desire.

Minerva.

Min.

When she looked over at him, her eyes widened, and the corners of her mouth turned down. "What are you doing here?"

"I came to check on you. Because you've been gone all day."

"I told you we would be," Minerva said. "I could think of nothing better to do while feeling safe than come to the beach."

That made him feel slightly guilty for terrorizing her last night.

"Have you been afraid of him all this time?"

"I… Yes," she said. "I had hoped that escaping would make him feel further away, but I was just waiting. Waiting for him to figure it out."

"Figure what out?"

She blinked. "Nothing."

"I know what it's like. To feel afraid all the time."

His mind was cast back to whom he'd been. That boy on the streets.

That boy who had held a gun to Robert King's head.

"It's terrible," she said softly.

"It is," he agreed.

He felt unkind that he had given her a false sense of what would happen in their marriage in the future. And now that he recognized she was so pleasing physically, there really was no question of them getting an annulment.

"Minerva, I know what it is to be afraid. I lived my life without security on the streets of Rome."

"I've been to Rome, and I can honestly say that now that statement means a lot more to me," she said.

"I'm sure it does. It is a terrifying thing to

have no control. Whether that be because of a lack of money, or because a person has decided to dismantle that. And when you figure out how to have power, you'll never go back. Not ever."

"I don't suppose."

"Then you will understand why there is no question of the two of us divorcing."

"What?"

"I'm solidifying this business deal with your father, the best way that I can. And if I were to divorce you it would cause problems."

"We talked about this. About... You helping me. And how he surely won't be angry with you if he knows that what you did you simply did to keep me safe."

"To a certain point. It is about consolidating power, Minerva. In my life I have always imagined that I'm building a wall between myself now and my past. Whenever I can build it stronger, build it higher, I will. This is such an opportunity, and I will take it."

He was not asking her for anything untoward, not in his mind.

It wasn't as if she were an innocent. She had a child.

"I will give Isabella my name," he said. "She will be my daughter. I can adopt her, legally. All of this can be accomplished once we are certain you're safe. Everything I own will be hers someday. And I will be her father."

The words sent a strange surge through his chest. "There are many things about family I don't understand. And I won't. I have been in yours for a great many years, and still... The foundation that is built beneath us during our earliest years matters a great deal. And I know that more than most. I can't promise I'll be the best father, but I will be better than the one that biology gave her. And I will be better than my own."

She picked Isabella up, in a move he now absolutely recognized. "And what about as a husband?"

"I will be good to you. Have I ever not been?"

"But will you ever love me?"

"You said yourself, Minerva, you don't

even like me very much. What do you care if I love you? You won't love me."

She bit her bottom lip. "Well, that's a pretty sad start to a marriage, don't you think?"

"No," he said. "I don't. The mutual interest of protecting your daughter, a desire to unite our family names... And you don't dislike me. Admit it."

"I will do no such thing," she sniffed. "You're old."

"Yes. I know. When I was a child I had to walk to the soup kitchen, in the snow, uphill both ways."

"Stop it," she said.

"I'm offering you security," he said. "I can offer you nothing that means more to me than that. Security is what I have built my entire new life on. And I will give it to you. You must understand what value that has to me. And with that I give you the greatest thing in my possession. It is better than love. Love is fickle and it breaks. Love destroys the moment that it malfunctions. I have seen it. My mother loved my father, and what did that get her? Years on the streets. Prostitution. She loved many men, and all they did was take from her. And that love that she felt for them gave them that power. It is a folly to love. Did you love Isabella's father?"

Her face took on a strange pallor. "No," she said. "I didn't."

"Well, then. I suppose there is no comparison for you to be had there. But by God, Minerva, you must know that what I would give you, what I would give her, is better than the potential of someday finding a relationship that could give you what? Will a man claim Isabella so wholly as his own? Or will he always make her feel second? Will he care so much about the interests of your family? As much as I do? Will he be able to keep you safe in the way that I have done?"

"And you'll do this... All for a business?"

There was something in her look that was beseeching, and he knew that she wanted another answer.

He had one. Much to his surprise.

"I see myself in Isabella. A vulnerable child. There is little outright good I have done in the world, but if I can spare her the realities of life, that harshness, until she must absolutely face it, then I will. I will be her wall against all that is behind her, all that would seek to harm her, and the brilliant future that she can have. I will be a man she can call father safely. I will not harm her."

Minerva's green eyes were glistening now. He knew that he had said the right thing.

"All right," she said, setting Isabella down on a blanket beneath the shade. "I agree. I'll be your wife. Really."

What shocked him most was the roaring in his ears. It took him a moment to realize that it wasn't the waves. That it was some kind of hot flood of triumph that was rallying through him like a river. He closed the distance between them, and pulled her into his arms, and then, he claimed her mouth for real.

Not because of their farce.

Not because there was an audience.

Because she was his wife.

And she was his.

CHAPTER NINE

MINERVA FELT LIKE she had come down with a terrible fever. She was hot all over, shaking, and her stomach felt like it was tossing and turning.

He was kissing her.

And it was different than the kiss that had happened at the engagement party. Different than the kiss at their wedding.

It was different than anything.

And she feared that she might be too. That somehow, between the revelations of last night, and this moment when his mouth had met hers, and all the in-between—those moments when he had made such a rational case for her being his wife permanently, and she had created a web of justification inside herself and pulled each gossamer strand tight, hoping that it would act as a safety net when she inevitably fell.

And fall she was doing.

Hard. Fast.

Into this deep, dark sensual kiss that kicked against her and made a mockery of what she had thought the day of their engagement party.

That she had thought it was in a kiss. Not a real kiss. For, a real kiss was supposed to make her feel light and airy, was supposed to fill her with joy.

But the feelings that she had for Dante were so much more complicated than that. A series of complications, in fact. That could never be so simple as a fantasy realized. Would that they could be. No, it was nothing like she had imagined because, of course, she hadn't taken into account that kissing involved another person.

Which meant that the movements were not all hers. Which meant that she wasn't in charge of how firm it was, of how deep it was.

And because there was another person involved, it was physical.

He was in a misty vapor of her fantasies

the way that it all materialized in her head when she was reading about a handsome heroic character that she might want to dream about.

Because Dante was real. Mortal. A man in the flesh, with hot skin and a pounding heart. With hard muscles and hard...

He pressed his hand to her lower back and drew her up against him. Hard.

Yes. All of him was hard.

He desired her. Whether or not it was because he was a man and he could desire whatever he chose at a given moment, or because he desired her specifically, she didn't know. But he did.

And that was... Intense and heady and frightening.

She also wanted to lean into it as much as she wanted to run from it. More than anything in the entire world. Why was nothing about this simple? Why wasn't it easy? Why did it feel world-ending and wonderful all at once?

When they parted, she knew.

She looked into his dark gaze and she knew that it was him.

Dante.

And she had no idea how she had come to be the one kissing him.

She, Minerva, who was nothing.

Not by comparison of her exceptional family. And certainly not in comparison with him.

She had done one vaguely heroic thing in her life, and that was take care of Isabella.

But then, she had to wonder if it was heroic at all, or if she had just been reacting.

Because what could you do when there was a little girl vulnerable and alone in the world, her mother was dead and the police were declining to investigate.

She could have allowed Isabella to go into foster care in Italy, but that would have only made her vulnerable to Carlo.

She would've bounced around and...

And Minerva would never have seen her again.

So Minerva had told the police that Isabella was her daughter.

And that was how it had continued.

Dante thought that she was at least interesting enough to have engaged in an affair with a mobster.

But she wasn't.

She had just been a witness to it, and that made her all the more bland.

She suddenly felt small and weak and trembling, and she hated herself for it.

"What's the matter?" He lifted his hand and dragged his thumb along her lower lip.

"Nothing," she said.

She lied because there was nothing else to do. She lied because all of this was a lie, so she might as well be one too.

"I think we had quite enough of the beach, don't you?"

"Have we?"

"Yes. You're my wife. And it's time to make that real."

"Oh… Well, it is real, in that it's legal."

"You know," he said, his voice lowering to a growl. "There were days when a marriage wasn't considered a marriage until it had been consummated."

"Right," she said. "Wasn't there some barbarous practice of hanging bloody sheets out the window to alert the nation of the purity of the bride?"

He chuckled. "Luckily," he said, "neither of us have to worry about your purity."

Her stomach fell.

"Luckily."

He bent down and picked up Isabella. With shaking hands, Minerva began to gather her things.

"Leave it," he said. "It will be dealt with later."

Min was half out of her mind by the time they tromped back up to the house, by the time Dante laid Isabella down in her crib and closed the door to the nursery behind him.

"Will she sleep?"

"She doesn't run on a schedule. She does what she does."

"But she is…due to sleep?" he asked.

If there was one thing that made Dante seem a little bit flummoxed, it was Isabella. Babies in general. And truly, she had managed to destroy some of his composure with her impromptu announcement about his being the father of her baby. She supposed that on some level she should be triumphant in that.

She might be relatively boring, but she had caused Dante Fiori a moment's concern. Had made that patrician brow crease for but a few seconds before he had taken control of the entire endeavor.

So she was several steps ahead of the rest of the world.

Maybe that made her not so boring.

But then, he thought that she was not a virgin. Thought that she might know something about how to please a man, and on that score he was going to be very disappointed.

"Do you really want me?" Her voice was small, and she despised it.

"Minerva," he said, his voice rough and hard. "Of all the things to come out of this ridiculous ruse of yours, the most disturbing is that I cannot look at you as I once did. I was content to leave you in the category of child. My friend's younger sister, the daughter of my mentor, but you insist on making yourself unique and singular. A woman who belongs only to yourself, and now, to me. I don't have a choice."

"You don't have a choice in what?"

"Wanting you. It is damned inconvenient, and I was content to stay immune to you. How… How have you made it so that I'm not? It makes no sense."

"Because I'm not your type," she said, feeling breathless.

"Not at all," he said, advancing on her. "I like women with dramatic curves, who wear makeup and style their hair." He reached out and took a lock of her own hair between his thumb and forefinger, rubbing it absently.

"I like women who respond to my touch with enthusiasm and not trepidation. I definitely don't like women who tell the world I have fathered their children and force me into a fait accompli. And yet somehow… Here we are."

He wrapped his arm around her waist and pulled her against his chest.

And they were right back where they'd been on the beach.

He wasn't just kissing her, he was consuming her. And she didn't know where she began and he ended. Didn't know what she wanted from all of this. Except that all she wanted was for it to keep going. For it to never stop.

No, kissing wasn't what she had imagined it might be. It was more. It was everything. It was physical. It consumed her. It made her doubt everything she had ever believed about herself and gave birth to entirely new ideas there on the spot.

It was magic. Dark, chaotic magic that she didn't know how to contend with. His hands didn't stay still. They roamed over her body, exploring dips and hollows in her spine, her waist, beneath her breasts.

He wasn't touching her anywhere outrageously intimate, and yet it almost seemed more scandalous for it.

She had been held in a man's embrace only one other time. And he had gone straight for the obvious places, his hand beginning to move to her breast even as his other hand had already moved down to grab her bottom.

She knew all about those obvious things, and she had found them so base and obvious they had contributed to the utter turnoff of the entire situation.

But Dante managed to take something base and elevate it. To make it feel like high art rather than simple pornography. It bewitched her. Mesmerized her. Made her into something she didn't recognize. But maybe that was a good thing.

Because she had never been all that entranced by what she did recognize inside herself. But he made her feel new.

He made her feel beautiful. And perhaps this would make it so.

He continued to kiss her, continued to explore her in that innocuous way that didn't feel innocuous at all.

She breathed in deep, inhaling the scent of him, the sensation of him as his mouth continued to move over hers.

Were they really going to have sex?

Was she really going to lose her virginity to Dante Fiori?

Her husband.

For a moment she was convinced that she

had escaped the real world and slipped in between the pages of a book.

Because this was something that would happen to one of her heroines, but not something that would happen to her. This deep, rich, exciting experience that was all tongue and teeth and glory.

The hands of the man whom she cherished most, no matter that she had tried to pretend she didn't.

The kiss was all fraught, endless glory, and she reveled in it.

Then, he picked her up, cradling her against him as he carried her past her bedroom and toward his.

She hadn't set foot in Dante's bedroom.

No, quite the contrary, she had avoided it.

Hadn't wanted anything to do with that.

But she could see now that it was because she did want something to do with it that she had avoided it quite so studiously.

These revelations about herself were coming too fast and on the heels of physical sensations that were far too new for her to fully understand them.

Why did she avoid the things she wanted most? Why did she bury them?

Why did she think she couldn't have these things?

She didn't know. Except that everyone had been so shocked by the fact that Dante was the father of her baby, that he wanted to marry her, that she knew on some level they all thought it too. That it was an accepted truth about Minerva to an extent.

Even though they loved her. Even though they supported her.

She was not now, nor had she ever been, considered a great and wonderful beauty.

And she had decided that meant she couldn't have things.

Had decided it meant she shouldn't try.

Even the way that she had been made up for the engagement party and the wedding had made her uncomfortable because she knew that people would compare her with Violet. She didn't want it.

But Dante wanted her. He was spreading her out on his large bed, and staring down at her with dark, keen eyes.

Then he stood back and stripped his shirt off, as he'd done the day before.

But the day before she hadn't been about to touch him. Hadn't been about to...

"Now you don't have to pretend that you aren't looking," he said.

"I would never pretend," Minerva said. "I don't have the kind of capacity to play games that many do. I'm honest."

But that was a lie. She wasn't honest. Of course Dante believed that she had experience with men. And she didn't.

But she wasn't about to tell him. It made the whole situation that much more precarious, made her connection to Isabella so much more tenuous.

"Well, then let me return your honesty with the same," he said.

He leaned over, grabbed the hem of her top and jerked it up over her head. Her nipples beaded in the cool air, a blush warming her against the chill. No man had ever seen her like this, and that this perfect specimen of one was staring at her now was more than a little bit embarrassing. But he looked... Well, he looked as entranced as she felt. And it made her feel... Something. Something so deep and intense, it made her want to cry. Made her want to turn away from him and turn toward him all at the same time.

She began to shake as he lowered himself down onto the bed, stretching his body over her.

His lips were a whisper away from hers, and all she wanted was for him to taste her again.

Because when his mouth was on hers, she couldn't think quite so well. And not being able to think was a gift.

She wanted to be carried away in the fantasy. She craved a little bit more gauze, a little bit of protection from this hard, physical reality. But she didn't know if she was going to be able to get any.

Not with him. Not with him so hard and real and large above her. Not with her heart threatening to pound out of her chest.

With her breath eluding her lungs.

A smile tilted up the corner of his mouth. That smile was... Wicked.

And she realized that she had never seen Dante like this before.

She had always found him beautiful. Formidable.

A tiger safely contained in an enclosure. She knew that he would never turn that focus, all that brilliant, amber glory, on to her. Knew that his fangs would be reserved for other quarry.

He had only ever protected her. But in doing that he'd concealed the most powerful parts of himself. Had hidden the true danger from her.

Except, now it was all focused on her. Deeply. Intensely.

Now, the tiger was looking at her as if she was going to be his next meal.

And here she was, lying down wantonly to be consumed.

He pushed the shorts he was wearing, discarding them quickly, and her mouth dried. She had never seen a naked, aroused man.

And the very first thing she wanted to say was that there was no way he would fit. On the heels of that came the hysterical urge to laugh. Because of course he thought she had given birth. In which case the size of a man's penis would be the smallest of concerns to her.

Though, his penis could never be called a small concern.

Yet again, she had to fight back the hysterical urge to laugh. Because it was either that or cry.

Either that or give in to the fear that was gripping her chest. No, it wasn't fear. Because she didn't want to run away. It was something deeper than that. Something that scraped at a raw edge in her heart. That call to deep emotion inside her that she didn't want to deal with or acknowledge.

That she wanted him to look at her and see beautiful.

That she wanted to be wrapped in his arms and held close, close to his body, and more than that to his heart.

That for her, this would never be a simple business deal, nor would it ever be a defense against the terrifying things out in the world. That for her, this was about feeling.

That for her, this would always be about her connection to him.

Because she couldn't have chosen another man.

She wouldn't have been able to imagine herself with another man.

She never would have been able to say the things she did to another man.

Just like she didn't want to kiss another man on that dance floor in Rome.

Because it was Dante. It always had been. And it always would be.

And that made her want to hide.

First of all because she was sure that he would see that shining out from her eyes. But second of all because she was absolutely convinced that she was reaching the highest, most brilliant peak of her life at the age of twenty-one. That she would never be able to have more or better than this moment.

Because at the end of it they would have to contend with reality. With what remained.

And perhaps he would be able to tell she'd never done this before, and perhaps he wouldn't. Maybe the farce would be over, and maybe it would not.

But whether or not she would be able to keep it up was another question entirely. Because once he had joined his body to hers...

Well. She would be new. She would be different. And she didn't know what would be waiting on the other side.

He grabbed hold of the waistband of her swimsuit bottoms and dragged them down her legs, leaving her exposed to his hungry gaze.

Yet again, he moved his hands to a place she didn't expect.

He pressed them against her hips, slid them upward, and then finally did he move his thumbs over her nipples. Back and forth. Stoking the heat in her body. Stoking desire in her soul.

He kissed her neck as he teased her there, kissed his way down her chest, pulling one beaded nipple into his mouth and sucking hard. And it was as if her universe now originated from there. As if she was nothing beyond that bright, white-hot point of sensation where his mouth met her body. He kissed her ribs, her belly button. Continued down her body until he grabbed hold of her thighs, wrapping his arms around her and tugging her down toward his mouth. And yet again he defied her expectations. He didn't ease her in with the touch of his fingers. No. Instead, his first contact with her most intimate area was with his tongue, sliding across her slick folds. Then he took that sensitized bud between her legs and sucked it between his lips, teasing and tormenting her with the tip of his tongue. She gasped, her bottom bowing up off the bed, and he took advantage of that to move his hands around to cup her there.

And then he held her up in place as he continued to torment her. As he continued to lavish pleasure on her until she couldn't breathe.

Until she didn't know herself. He had transformed her into a begging, weeping creature of need.

And this was what she had always feared. Truly, deep in her heart, she had feared this. That she would be debased before him. That she wanted him so much would be revealed and so easily.

She wanted him. No woman twisting and sobbing in the arms of a man, on the verge of orgasm from a few strokes of his tongue over her most intimate flesh, could pretend that she didn't have feelings for him.

No woman could pretend that she was dispassionate when she wasn't horrified by such an act, but craved more. Reveled in the intimacy of it. In the intensity. And then, he added a finger to his pleasuring. Pressed one digit deep inside her before adding another.

She felt herself begin to stretch. She felt like she was going to fly apart. Like it was too much. Like this was too much. How would she ever be able to accommodate the rest of him if two fingers pushed the edges of reason for her body?

Except all she knew was that she wanted more. Whether or not she was convinced she could handle more.

She wanted him. She wanted him even if it made no sense. She wanted him even if she would cry. Even if it would cause her pain.

What a strange thing. That a woman must want a man so much the first time that she would willingly submit herself to that pain. That invasion.

That a woman must have a physical marker of her virginity in a physical cost for losing it.

But she was willing. She was willing to pay the cost.

And when he made his way back up her body, as she was spent from her first climax and his mouth met hers, treating her to absolute evidence of her own need for him. Of the intensity of it.

And yet, she wasn't ashamed. To the contrary, she was spurred on.

Because she did want him. She couldn't pretend she didn't. And maybe that was the key.

Minerva had little to offer him. But she had herself. All the desire in the world. And the purity of her need for him was real.

She could give him that. And perhaps that was something he had never gotten from those practiced, beautiful socialites whom he was accustomed to.

An authenticity of need.

Maybe…

Maybe there was a gift in her innocence. In all that she was. Maybe that she had no skills or tricks or trinkets to offer him was a gift in and of itself.

"I'll go slow," he said, his voice rough.

And she realized that he intended to go slow because he thought she was only three months out from having given birth.

Not that she was a virgin.

But perhaps that would help.

When the thick, blunt head of him probed her untried flesh, she winced, and when he began to inch inside her she cried out. Gritting her teeth as he met the resistance that she knew signaled her inexperience.

And then, he had breached her. It hurt. Terribly.

And there was no way she could pretend it didn't. She cried out, and cursed herself as ten times the fool that she had ever thought for believing that she could hide this from him.

He began to withdraw and she panicked,

grabbing hold of his rear end urging him back in.

"No," she said. "We have to. I need you."

He began to ease forward again, the effort it was taking him to go slow visible in the way the cords stood out on his neck.

"Please," she beseeched him.

And on a growl he thrust all the way home.

She had not been prepared. For the intensity of this. For the invasion of this.

For his rampant masculinity in the way that it would utterly and completely demolish her softness.

Her femininity.

For the fact that it was like a conquering.

But one she had surrendered to. Willingly. Joyously.

His dark eyes met hers, his expression that of a fierce warrior. His mouth moved, as though he was about to speak, and she stretched up, capturing the words with her lips, swallowing them. Because she didn't want to talk about anything right now. She didn't want to inhabit reality.

All she wanted was this.

For him to inhabit her. For him to take her and remake her, so that she was new. And maybe, maybe parts of him would become new too. Maybe they could do that for each other. Maybe.

He growled against her mouth, but he didn't try to speak to her again. Instead, he began to move.

Hard and fast, establishing a rhythm that left her breathless.

That carried them both up to the stars.

And when she shattered there up among the heavenly bodies, she finally felt like she belonged.

Like she was beautiful.

Beautiful in his arms. Beautiful for him.

Crying out her pleasure with no shame at all.

And when he tipped over the edge, a roar of pleasure coming from deep inside him, she held him. While he shook. While he poured himself out inside her.

She had never felt so female. She had never felt so powerful. Wrapped around this hard, muscular body that might have been carved out of rock were it not for the heat that radiated off him.

Were it not for the way he breathed. Hard and jagged as though something had been broken inside him.

When it was finished, he rolled away, and looked at her. His eyes were unreadable. Unfathomable.

And she couldn't guess what he would say next.

But she also couldn't contain the lie inside her anymore.

Whether he had guessed or not.

Based on the expression there, she had a feeling that he didn't know what he might have guessed or not.

But she wouldn't make him guess. She wouldn't make him speculate. There was no place for that with them.

"I didn't give birth to Isabella," she said.

And by the way the mountain moved, she could tell that he hadn't been close to guessing that at all.

CHAPTER TEN

DANTE WAS STILL reeling from the ecstasy that he had found in Minerva's arms. He had been ready to lecture her on allowing him to hurt her while her body was still tender, and then she had dropped that bombshell on him. And it made him go back in time. Every moment, every kiss, every touch since they had embarked on this farce.

The moment that he had first entered her body and she had flinched.

It was impossible.

It couldn't be.

That she was not an innocent was one of the only reasons that he could have justified demanding that she become his wife in body as well as in name.

He had been certain that she had known exactly what he was demanding of her.

But she did not.

And while he didn't hold to medieval ideas about virginity, and he was certainly not going to go hang a sheet out the window, it was about his age. His experience. The fact that he had swept her off the beach and taken her practically straight to bed without…

She had wanted it. He was certain of that.

But how could he be sure that she knew what she had wanted?

And how dare she lie to him?

Because he had been embroiled in this entire situation against his will, and apparently, Isabella was not her daughter.

Which begged the question… Who was the child?

And whom was Minerva actually hiding her from?

"Dammit," he said, moving to a sitting position. "Have you stolen this child?"

"No!" Minerva scrambled to a sitting position, clutching the sheets to her breasts. The entire left side of her body was still completely bare, and his eyes were drawn to that golden skin that he knew now was softer than he could have anticipated.

And he had no reason to be staring at her now. Not when he was looking at a traitor.

She had lied to him.

"Then explain this," he said. "Explain this entire thing. She's not your child?"

"Not biologically," Minerva said. "I said I didn't give birth to her. I didn't say I wasn't her mother."

"You adopted her?" he pressed.

"Not exactly. I lied. And everything... Everything to do with her birth was a disaster." She pressed her hands to her temples. "I have to start at the beginning."

"You had better."

"You know when I left for school I was planning on doing a new country each year, a new university. Right. Well, when I went to Rome I was rooming with a woman named Katie. She was also from the States. We didn't know each other before, but we became friends. She was very different from me."

Minerva clasped her hands in front of her and made a study of them. "I liked her. I was fascinated by her. Mostly because I'd never known anyone like her. I know everyone thinks that Maximus and Violet are wild because they go to parties all the time. But nobody as successful as they are isn't working most of the time."

Minerva lifted a shoulder. "I was studying, mostly. And Katie was in and out at all hours. Finally, I agreed to go out with her one night. We went to a club down in Rome. We met men."

A dark anger welled up in his chest. "But you didn't. You didn't have sex with him. You were a virgin."

He didn't know why now he felt the need to confirm that. And why the idea that this other man might have done something with her angered him.

"He kissed me once," Minerva said. "I didn't like it. I told him I wanted to leave. But Katie didn't want to leave, because she had met someone and she wanted to go home with him. I went back to our dorm by myself. The next morning, she came home, and she was in a good mood. She liked Carlo. She wanted to keep seeing him."

"And then what?"

"She started realizing he wasn't a good man. She tried to pull away. And it seemed to work. He seemed to lose interest. Then she changed. She started seeming more depressed than wild. That was when she told me she was pregnant. And we had to hide it from him. She said he was dangerous, and that was why she had left him. But like I said, it seemed as if he had lost interest in her. But he came to visit one day months later, and he saw that she was pregnant, and he said he wanted the baby. She told him no. We called the police. But..."

"Connections within crime families extend far. I know."

"We hoped that we were safe. After she had Isabella, she slid into a depression. Only two weeks after Isabella was born she started using drugs. I mean, she had always used them, but when she went out for the night. Not at home, and not during her pregnancy. But she was paranoid, and she was anxious, and she needed something to calm her down. I quit going to class too." She looked down at her hands. "I was so worried about her. I was so worried about Isabella."

She took a breath and forged on. "I took care of her, like she was my baby. It just… happened one day. I decided I couldn't do half. And since Katie couldn't do it at all, I just did. I fed her, clothed her, rocked her to sleep." She blinked hard. "One day I went out shopping with Isabella, and when I came back there were police at our apartment. Katie was… Her body was gone already. They said that she had died of a drug overdose. But I was afraid that wasn't true."

Min's eyes met his, and the green fire there was intense. "I will always be afraid that isn't true. That he wanted the baby. I told the police Isabella was mine. And then the very next day I packed up and I left Italy. I came back home with her. And then he found me. I wanted him to believe that Isabella was my baby. I wanted to… Cast doubt on it. Because I'm sure that he never paid enough attention to me to know whether or not I might have been pregnant. In fact, I doubt he ever would have recognized me no matter how many times he saw me. I'm plain, after all. But I think he found out who was rooming with her, and he began a search. I think he can't be certain that Isabella is his, and I'm counting on that. I was counting on you standing with me. Because I never slept with him either. So if... If I have a baby. If I have one with you..."

Helpless rage coursed through him, because what could he say? He had been lied to. But Minerva had been doing the very best she could.

There had been nothing else.

And he would never have suggested another plan. There was nothing else. She was correct in that. Claiming the child for her own was brilliant, and using him was brilliant in ways he hadn't understood.

"He doesn't believe you, though," he said.

"He doesn't know, though," she said. "I'm sure of that. He's not completely certain. I don't think he ever saw Isabella. I don't think he can be sure if Katie had the baby. Only that there was a baby in our apartment."

"But you know he wants her anyway."

"Yes. And if he does any test then he'll know for sure that she's his. I fear that if he did a test and found out she wasn't he would have simply…"

"He doesn't care for anyone or anything," Dante said. "Men like that don't. Men who don't value life don't value life of any sort."

"She's in danger. And so am I." Min swallowed hard. "I think he had her killed, Dante. I do. I can't prove it, and maybe the police covered it up. But what would he do to her? What would he expose her to? And me? Well, he'd just get rid of me, wouldn't he?"

"You didn't make that clear enough," Dante said. "I'm going to make sure he's dealt with."

"Please," Minerva said. "Please don't…"

"I'm not going to have them killed. But I am going to finance operations to destroy that crime family. And I think I have the connections in Rome to do it. It will all have to be done at once, and it will require money they likely don't possess. The problem is you have to get everyone within law enforcement on his payroll at the same time."

She nodded slowly. "Right and that... That's difficult."

He shook his head. "Difficult is coming up from the streets of Rome. Starting out the son of a prostitute and becoming a billionaire. That is difficult. This just takes the right moves at the right time, and the right amount of money. And it will be done."

He stared down at her, at his wife. He had made her his wife in truth, and he could never go back on it. Minerva was his wife, and her protection was his responsibility.

He had grown up on the streets among men like Carlo.

He knew that his father was likely a man quite like him.

And this was his opportunity to do more than simply build another brick in the wall of his own security.

But to knock down the wall that separated an organized crime family from justice.

And he would do it.

For Minerva. For Isabella.

For the boy whom he'd once been.

This was all he could do. At the end of the day, it was the only thing.

He would be a father who protected Isabella. A husband to protect Minerva.

God knew he didn't have anything else to offer.

CHAPTER ELEVEN

TIME SEEMED TO move differently on the island. It went in a haze, long leisurely days, gourmet food and sunshine. And then at night Dante made love to her.

She had the sense that he was angry with her for the deception, but he also hadn't turned away from her. She half expected him to. After the revelation that she'd been a virgin, she had expected that he might find her… She didn't know.

But time and time again he showed her that he didn't find her to be a problem. That he was attracted to her. That he wanted her.

And she wondered why that still didn't feel like enough.

She had never imagined that a man like him would find her compelling in the first place. And he did. Shouldn't she be happy with that? Shouldn't she, the less attractive sister, be happy with the crumbs that she was being handed?

Well, it didn't really matter. Because what they had was what they had.

And on the island it was only the two of them anyway. And whatever insecurity she felt about taking this into the real world...

She didn't doubt Dante's commitment. Not in the least. He was a man who would keep his word, she was certain of that.

But what she was less certain of was his feelings. Those... Those were unknowable. Utterly and completely. Today, she had talked him out of simply working in the office and had badgered him down to the beach. Often, she and Isabella spent their time there alone. Dante was a workaholic, though she was exposed to enough billionaires to know that you didn't build empires without being married primarily to your job. But still, she felt lonely.

And then she had to wonder if she was being selfish. Because wasn't she with her dream man? How could she want anything more?

Isabella began to fuss where she was lying

on the towel, and she turned to Dante. "Can you pick her up?"

He looked stiff.

"She's our daughter now," she said. "Yours as much as mine."

"Meaning not?" he asked, his tone hard.

She looked at him for a long moment, trying to gauge that statement. What it meant to him.

"No," she said, slowly. "Meaning she very much is."

"Blood matters," he said.

She narrowed her eyes and studied him. "Why do you think that?"

If he noticed her careful appraisal, he didn't acknowledge it. "Because."

"You think that blood is more important than caring for a child. That blood trumps love?"

"No. I don't suppose I thought of it that way."

"But you think it matters."

"Of course it does," he said. "After all, your father didn't offer the company to me, not until I was engaged to marry you."

"Did you expect him to?"

"He always says that I'm like a son to him," Dante said. "But it's not the same."

"It very much is," Minerva said. "He loves you."

"And I'm a brother to you?"

Her cheeks heated. "Of course you're not the same as my brother. But that's the problem. You never have been. Not to me. You too… Well, I hear tell that my brother's beautiful, and I suppose that I'm proud of him in that way that a sister is. But I don't see his beauty, not in that way. Yours I could never unsee."

"Did you really have a crush on me when you were young?"

"I'm still young," she sniffed. "And you're changing the subject."

"What, you want to turn the subject back to something that's upsetting you? I don't know very much about marriage, Minerva, but I know enough to know that I shouldn't aim to upset my wife."

"I was willing to put my life at risk for her," Minerva said. "I am willing to do that.

I was willing to uproot my entire life for her. Tell me, do you think that that needs blood to be more intense? Is there anything more intense? I would fix everything in her life if I could. I would vanquish all of her enemies. All of them. I hate that she's been exposed to threats. I hate that someone would harm her. Please, tell me, Dante, if you think her biological father loves her more than I do."

"Enough," he said. "This is a useless fight. The concept of family... It's good she has you. That you're willing to do that. For my part, I offer what I can."

"They say blood is thicker than water," she said. "I know they say that. But in my opinion blood can be dangerous. Blood can stain. It is not about the blood in your veins. The heart pumps the blood, after all. Isn't the heart the most important thing?"

"No," he said. "The heart is not most important. It is your brain that will serve you well, Minerva. It is your brain that you need."

"Your brain?"

"Your brain is capable of great compassion. Of rationalizing what the safest and best thing is to do. Your brain was fully engaged, your sense of duty when it comes to humanity. To tell you the truth, I don't believe even blood creates a family."

"What holds my family together, then?" she asked.

He made an exasperated sound. "Your father has a strong sense of civic duty. Something that I will now employ, something I will pay back with Isabella."

"You think *civic duty* is what holds society together?" she asked incredulously. "That is the most depressing thing I have ever heard."

"Yes," he said. "I do."

"You think… Swiss Family Robinson survived and built a house on an island because of civic duty? Or did they… Did they put their hearts into it?"

"That's more than a clumsy metaphor and *Swiss Family Robinson* is fictional."

"We learn from fiction, don't we? To see ourselves? The world? Our hearts?"

"Our hearts want things that are bad for us, Minerva. Witness your friend and Carlo. Carlo is another prime example of people who have corrupt hearts. Tell me, what can we count on to guide us with evidence such as this?"

"Love," she said. And it was clear, simple and concise to her. That love was what separated these things. That love was what made people choose someone else over themselves. Time and time again.

"Love," he said, the word a sneer. "Do you know what my mother loved?" he said. "Drugs."

"I thought that your mother… I thought that she was a prostitute to help support you."

"She was a prostitute to help support her cocaine habit."

He looked out at the horizon. And there was something so bleak and desolate in his dark eyes that she felt wounded by it.

"Dante, I'm sure that she loved you."

He shook his head, his lip curling up into a sneer. "Do you want to know one of my most vivid memories of my mother?"

"Yes," she said, knowing for sure that she didn't, because she could sense that there was nothing but pain in his next words.

"One of my very first memories of my mother was on her last birthday. I was eight years old. But I already knew how to cook for myself. I already knew how to cook for us. I had taken the money that she kept in our cookie jar, and I took it to market. With that I bought all of this, and I bought cheese. I bought bread. Pasta. I bought a feast, because I wanted to celebrate her birthday. There was cake. We never had cake. But it was for her, so I felt that it was okay. And when she got home, do you know what she said to me?"

He looked at her, his dark gaze unwavering. "She said, *'You stupid boy.'* And then she slapped me across my face."

Minerva clutched at her chest, her heart nearly folding in on itself. "No," she whispered.

"Yes. She said that she was going to have to go out and earn more money on her back to buy what she really needed for her birthday. It wasn't dinner with me, just so you know. It was more of her drug. She loved that more than she ever loved me. She took care of me out of a sense of obligation, and this is where

I come back to duty, because thank God she did. Otherwise, she might have left me somewhere to die. Instead..."

He cut off his words.

"Dante," she said. "I'm sorry. But you must know that's not... That's not how it's supposed to be. Not in a healthy family."

"Really? And tell me, Minerva, in your healthy family, how is your sense of who you are? How is your sense of self when compared to everyone else?"

"I can't help it I was born into a family of overachievers," she said.

"I suppose not. But I'm just saying. Your family is among the most loving I've ever known, and can you honestly tell me they haven't given you issues of some kind? Love doesn't erase all of the issues out there in the world."

"I never said it did," she said.

"No, but on some level I think you believe it might."

"Wouldn't it be a nice thing to believe?"

"I'm not sure where that would leave my life."

She nodded slowly. Then she rose up from where she was sitting and crossed to him, pressing her hand to his bare chest and stretching up on her toes, kissing him slowly. Usually when they came together, there was an urgency to it. He was extremely conscious of her inexperience, and it had taken her a while to figure out how she felt about that.

Because the first time he had been considerate, but he had treated her like she knew what she was doing.

He had a tendency now to treat her like glass.

But still, they didn't linger over these sorts of kisses.

He braced his hand against her hip and held her as they did, and she felt warmth flood her body. An ache. A need that went beyond sexual. And when they parted she looked into his eyes, and she tried to see something. Anything. Caring. A connection.

She couldn't read it. She couldn't read him.

"Dante, you can have whatever life you want. You're a billionaire."

A small smile touched his lips and he

brushed his thumb over her cheekbone. "Do you get all your ideas from books, Minerva? Or have you lived any of your own life at all?"

The words were said softly enough, but they were designed to pierce her chest.

They were designed to reinforce the fact that she was younger. That whatever she thought or felt, it would never be right, not in his eyes, because he knew more, had experienced more.

It wasn't fair.

And he knew it.

She turned away from him and went back and picked Isabella up. "It's fine," she said. "And yes, Dante, I have experienced things in life. You know, the death threats. Making the choice to be a mother to Isabella. And when I made that choice, by the way, I didn't make it thinking that it would be temporary. Thinking that all he would do was offer her base protection over her life. I knew that I was giving myself to her. To this. Maybe I understand more things than you think."

It was only when she had reached the relative safety and sanity of the house that she realized he had succeeded in derailing the conversation, even if she was the one who had left it on a good parting shot.

He was uncomfortable talking about family.

And given what his mother had done to him, she did understand. But it had nothing to do with her or Isabella. And none of it did anything to soothe the longing inside her. For this to be real. He'd said that she was going to be his wife in truth, but he didn't mean it. Not in the way that she recognized it. He meant sex.

And the sex was lovely, she wouldn't pretend that it wasn't. But for her all it had done was open up a deeper desire inside her. It satisfied nothing.

Because there was only one aspect of them that was engaged in it. Or rather, one aspect of him. His body. Not his heart.

And she wanted…

She wanted it. His heart.

She was perilously close to being in love with her husband.

He saw her. Whether clothed or naked, on the beach or in the kitchen, their bedroom, he saw her. And she had spent a lifetime feeling very unseen.

He wanted her.

And most of all, he had pledged to protect her, and to protect Isabella.

He had been protecting her for years.

Picking her up when she scraped her knees. Rescuing her from humiliation on a dance floor.

Oh, yes, there was a lot to love about that man.

The realization made her gasp. Because she could think of nothing lonelier. Nothing sadder than a life spent loving someone passionately, pouring out your desire, your body, to them and getting a hollow facsimile in return.

She would love Isabella. And Isabella would love her back. And Dante would be her father.

He was right... He was right that with him she would have something much better than Carlo. She wasn't being robbed of anything there.

And Dante could not withhold his heart

from his daughter. Whatever he said, Minerva knew that. Isabella was a baby, and babies existed to be loved by those who cared for them. Those who were not violent criminals anyway. Which Dante was not.

She was another matter.

But she was always another matter.

And she had Isabella to consider, which meant she would have to remain another matter altogether.

And she would have to find a way to be fine with it.

Three mornings later Dante was informed that Carlo had been killed in a shootout with police. The members of his crime family, including the top boss, had all been taken into custody, as had three members of the police department who were on the payroll.

It was the largest such operation to be completed in years. Dante and his money were largely seen as being responsible.

But all Dante saw was an opportunity to get back to his real life. To get back to the real world.

And it was time.

He was tempted to forget himself here on this island with Minerva. Tempted to get lulled into a sense that life began and ended here. The white sand to the line of the crystal blue ocean.

The longer they were here, away from life, the easier it was to forget who he was. The easier it was to let Min fill his vision and forget that there was reality waiting for them both.

But he had work back in New York, and he had to see to those things. Had to remember who he was.

Minerva was in her room. It was strange to him that she had opted to keep her own bedroom, especially considering she slept in his bed every night. But her things were still in the white room by Isabella's. And she was holed up in there reading a book. He startled her when he pushed the door open. "Carlo is dead."

"He is?" She sat up, eyes wide, and there was a kind of glittering triumph in her expression. Then it softened. "You didn't…"

"I didn't. It happened when the police tried to take him into custody. There was nothing for it. But either way. You're safe."

"Does that mean we're going home?"

"Yes," he said. "We're going home." She let out a whoop, which surprised him, and leaped across the space, into his arms.

He stood there, unmoving for a moment, and then wrapped his arms around her.

He never knew quite what to do with her.

"I thought you liked it here," he said.

She separated from him. "I do," she said, her cheeks turning pink. "But…"

"Yes. It's rather isolated."

"Yes. It's just… As beautiful as it's been, I miss normal life. Isabella deserves normal."

"Well, you did marry a billionaire. Normal may not exactly be in the cards."

She laughed and shook her head. "Fine. I'll take your normal."

She smiled, and it tugged something in his chest. "We'll leave immediately."

"I guess I should get packed…"

"No need. Everything will be waiting for

us when we get to our home. And anything you need here will be sent."

"Oh."

"The pilot is already on his way."

They were in the sky only an hour later.

Minerva was beginning to seem agitated.

"Why are you picking at your fingernails?"

"I'm not," she said, pulling at her finger.

"You are." He put his hand over hers. "What are you doing?"

She stopped then. "Nothing."

"Something."

"We didn't discuss… Dante, I know that you have a terrible reputation for being a womanizer. And you… You treat me like I'm fragile. You treat me like you might break me when we're in bed."

He was taken aback by her frankness, but he let her go on.

"I don't know any kind of bedroom tricks. There are always magazine saying there are one hundred sex tips in there. I don't even think I know two." She wrinkled her nose. "Well, no. I do. I might know three. But even then, they're not very well developed. And it

was one thing when we were on the island
and there were no other women. But are you
going to… Are you going to get tired of me?"

"We said vows," he said. "I will not vio-
late them."

She wrinkled her nose. "That isn't answer-
ing my question."

"Didn't you want to know if I was going to
be faithful?"

"Well, yes. But I also want to know if you're
going to be *bored*."

"I can have the same concern, Minerva.
You've only been with one man. How do I
know that you won't get resentful of that fact?
That you won't want to try someone different. To experience variety."

"I won't," she said.

"Very confident. All the confidence of the
inexperienced."

"No," she said. "It's that I had opportunity
in my life, and I didn't take it. It took me all
this time to realize it was because of you. Because of how I felt about you. That I… That
I was attracted to you."

"Right. But now you know what it is to be with me. Perhaps the mystery is gone."

"It was never about mystery," she said.

"How about we simply both promise each other fidelity."

"Okay," she said softly.

And he could tell that he had done something wrong, but he wasn't certain what.

It was clear he had done another thing wrong when the plane began to touch down several hours later and Minerva let out a gasp. "Where are we?"

"I told you, we are going home."

"This is not home. This is… Manhattan."

"I live in Manhattan," he said.

"I don't," she said. "I live in San Diego."

"Not anymore," he said, feeling irritated now.

"You just assume that home would be your home."

"And you assume that home would be yours."

"Well… Well…"

"And I am the one with the private jet, so really, I was the only one that wasn't making assumptions, but had charted a course. If I were you, I would have checked if I was uncertain."

"I was not uncertain!"

"Well, clearly you should have been."

She huffed inelegantly. "Dante, this isn't going to work if you just think you can run around making all the decisions for me."

"I didn't make a decision for you. You didn't ask what decision was being made."

"You're infuriating. Somehow, I forgot that on the island. It was all the kissing."

"Well. I am good at kissing, even though I am infuriating."

"I miss my *family*," she said.

He didn't know why, but that word family caught him in his chest just then.

But of course she did. She missed Robert and Maximus, Violet and Elizabeth.

They were her family.

They were her blood.

"We will go and visit," he said. "And I promise you I will look into buying a home there. But my business is largely conducted out of Manhattan, and that is where we will be."

"And when you join with my father?"

"I imagine it won't change. As long as he is running things on the West Coast, I will be of more use to him here."

"I don't want to live in New York," she said, frowning deeply.

"You have something against it?" He looked out the window at the gray. Gray sea. Gray skyline.

"Please," she said. "It snows here."

"It's not like snow is imminent," he said.

"It's so busy."

"Wait to pass judgment until you've seen our home."

She kept her peace, at his request, and she only stared wide-eyed out the car window as they drove through the streets of Manhattan heading toward his penthouse apartment.

Then, she continued to be silent as they migrated to the building and went up in the gold elevator that carried them to the very top of the high-rise.

"This does not seem like a very good place to raise a child," she said.

"We are not in the penthouse yet," he said.

"We're in the elevator. It's adjacent."

"You must reserve your opinion until you see it."

"I mustn't *do anything*," she said, sounding crabby.

"You know, *cara*," he said, "many people are afraid of me."

"I suppose those people don't have any experience of you dancing with them to spare you humiliation at a party."

"Your father clearly expected it."

She bared her teeth, and he would have been amused by her show of anger if he weren't… compelled. And he didn't know what he felt compelled to do or why. She reached into places inside of him and…did that thing that Min did.

She couldn't leave well enough alone, not ever.

"Fine, then," she said. "I suppose those people also don't have experience of them marrying them so that you can protect a baby."

"That isn't the only reason I married you."

"It isn't?"

"No. I did want a share in your father's business."

He knew that that was unkind. He knew that it was the worst thing to say to her, and yet he'd said it anyway. Her entire frame sagged. But then, the doors to the elevator slid open and it revealed the grand penthouse. Dark, marble floors and a grand view of Central Park.

"Those windows don't open, do they?"

"No," he said.

"It's very strange being so high up."

"You act like a country mouse. You were raised in California."

"Yes. And San Diego is the city. But not like this. This is *The City*."

"Yes. That's why I like it." Perhaps *like* was a strong word, but he appreciated the way that New York effectively drowned out his thoughts and memories. It was like a comforting white noise that followed you everywhere you went. So busy, so consumed with its own self, that it left you little time to reflect.

"I won't like it," she said resolutely.

"You've been here many times, and you do like New York."

"To visit," she said. "I love to see the Christmas tree in Rockefeller Center. And I love tea. Everywhere. I love the museums. But I've never wanted to live here."

"Isn't it a shame, then," he said, drawing the words out, "that you married me?"

Furious eyes met his. "I'm beginning to think so."

A muscle in his cheek ticked. "Do you wish to keep your own room here?"

"Yes," she returned.

He gritted his teeth. "Fine. You will find it is the second door on the left, and I believe clothes have been moved in for you."

"You knew that I wanted my own room."

"You kept one on the island."

A strange wave passed between them, a question that she didn't ask, and one that he didn't press.

"I'm going into my office."

"Where is that? Which room?"

"Not an office here. I must go into the office. We were gone for so long, and before that I was already in San Diego. Everything has been handled in my absence, but I need to make an appearance."

"You just got here."

"Yes. But you are in New York. I'm sure that you can find something to occupy yourself."

The man he'd been on the island wasn't the man he was in truth, and the sooner Minerva learned that the better.

There was no place for tenderness or pity inside him.

No place for hope.

He knew that those things only brought about destruction. And he would never allow himself to be destroyed again.

And without a backward glance, Dante walked back out of the penthouse, leaving Isabella and Minerva behind him.

CHAPTER TWELVE

THEY WERE IN a strange standoff that Minerva couldn't quite decode. She had slept in her bedroom for the last three nights, and he hadn't come to her. On the island sex was how they'd communicated. And maybe that wasn't healthy, but it had provided some sort of closeness at least.

This confirmed that her decision to ambush him about the sex on the plane was valid. She'd had the sense if she didn't say it there, she wouldn't have the chance.

Almost as if she knew that once they were in this great gray city it would all be changed.

It was.

And she was oppressed by the gray. Emotionally and all around them. Even the view of Central Park felt gray.

And maybe out of sheer stubbornness she had not gone out of the apartment to explore the city. He was right, it was New York and there were endless things to do. But Isabella was still small, and Minerva was conscious of the various illnesses that lurked out there on every park bench, handrail and shopping cart.

At least, that was what she told herself.

And she did not allow herself to think that maybe she was just being stubborn.

That she was refusing to accept her new life out of sheer spite. Because she didn't want to be in this.

And why? She wasn't entirely sure.

It wasn't like she hadn't left home before. She had. On her grand adventure to Rome— which had ended up containing a little bit of disaster.

She swallowed hard.

Mostly, she was a little bit grateful for this strange coolness between them.

It had allowed her some time to regroup.

On the island she had been convinced that she was in love with him. Or at least, mostly in love with him. Here, she could see that it had been a combination of sun and sex. Here, she could see that she was inexperienced, and was responding to him in that way.

That she had been afraid of leaving the island in part because she had known that it would affect a change in their relationship.

That losing the cocoon of intimacy that had surrounded them there would thrust them back into the real world, and she would have to contend with the fact that marriage vows neither of them had particularly meant would not create an unbreakable bond.

Neither would they create feelings where they didn't exist. At least, not on his hand.

But it was fine. Because her feelings had been magnified.

She had to accept that she had a crush on Dante, and now that she was working it out she had a bit of clarity.

When he returned home that night, his expression was stern. "Three dresses are being sent, and the nanny will be here shortly."

"Nanny?"

"Yes. The nanny that you were using back in San Diego is on a plane on her way here. We have an engagement to go to tonight."

"We do?"

"Yes. A gala. As I didn't know if I would be back in the city I hadn't committed to it, but as it is, it's a connection that your father would very much like me to make. It is in the interest of King, and given that, it is important that you come with me."

"So, my father has been in touch with you? He hasn't been in touch with me." She could have easily been in touch with her family. But she was in high avoidance mode. Feeling fragile and not wanting to deal with the realities of her family, now that she married and slept with Dante, and she didn't want to hear anything about the news reports on them either.

She wanted to hide in this apartment. And she wanted to be home.

She didn't make any sense even to herself.

And she was far too wrung out to care.

"We had business to discuss."

"Well. I'm glad to know business is so important." She felt wholly shunted off to the side, which wasn't fair at all. She didn't care.

"Minerva," he said. "Being my wife is a

role. I apologize if you didn't realize that, but you took the vows. You needed me to fulfill my end of the brief, and I have done it. Additionally, I am acting as Isabella's father."

"You're not acting as her father. You are her father."

For the first time she was starting to worry he might not bond with her. She'd taken his reluctance as a typical reaction from a man who had no experience with babies. Now she was a bit concerned about the distance. Which was beginning to seem resolute.

"Fine," he said. "According to the paperwork that we will soon process, I am her father."

The distance in those words kicked against Minerva's heart. "Yes," she said drily.

"And you are my wife. What I need from a wife is someone to come to events on my arm and look appropriately adoring at me. I need you to help enhance my image. I most particularly need you to do this as I act on behalf of King. It would not do for me to be seeing to this business and having you looking dour beside me. You know what people would say."

"The truth? That it's a marriage of convenience?"

"It is a decidedly inconvenient marriage," he said. "And I would like it to be more convenient."

"It didn't seem so inconvenient to you when you had sex on tap."

"Who turned the tap off?"

"I was under the impression it was mutual."

She sniffed off to her room in a huff and fed Isabella. Then, when the dresses arrived, so did the nanny, and she was overjoyed to be reunited with the baby.

Minerva felt slightly annoyed by it, but she was happy that Isabella would be with someone familiar.

The dresses were beautiful. Far too beautiful for her. There was a note pinned to one of them. From Violet.

Minerva nearly burst into tears, and she picked up her phone and dialed her sister's number. "The dresses are wonderful," she said.

She couldn't put on a front, not now.

She didn't have the strength to. Violet had breached her hiding place, and she couldn't be angry. She wanted to connect to someone too badly.

"What's wrong?" Violet asked.

"It's a disaster," Minerva said. "We're at each other's throats. He's not speaking to me hardly at all and he's not… Well, he's not anything and I miss him and I shouldn't. It's not fair! I didn't ask for this part of it!"

"I don't understand…"

The whole story came pouring out of Minerva. She didn't want secrets between herself and her sister. She desperately needed an ally, and whatever issues she had with Violet were her own. Her own smallness. Her own feelings of inadequacy.

"Wow," Violet said. "I mean… Minerva," she said. "That is the bravest thing I've ever heard of."

She sniffed, sitting on the edge of the bed, feeling worn down. Brave was the last thing she felt. "I don't know if I was very brave."

"Yes, you were. Why do you have such a

hard time taking credit for the good things that you do?"

She picked at the velvet fabric on the duvet cover. "Because they're nothing. Nothing compared to the kind of things that you and Maximus do."

"I manufacture makeup," Violet said drily. "And I sell it very effectively. But I've never saved anyone's life." Minerva was distinctly uncomfortable with that statement.

"You're amazing," Minerva said. "Don't minimize it."

"We are talking about *you*," Violet said. "And you can't even handle a compliment when you're the topic of conversation."

"Vi," Minerva said. "You shouldn't have to talk yourself down to try and make me feel better."

"I'm not," Violet said. "Trust me, Minerva, my sense of self is pretty well developed. But you're clearly lacking in perspective."

"I just…" Min fell onto her back and gazed up at the ceiling. Even from this perspective the light seemed gray. "He doesn't love me.

He never even slept with me. I mean…before all this started."

"You have now." It was more of a confirmation request than a question.

"Yes," Minerva admitted. "I did have feelings for him. I mean, like a crush. You remember what he did for me at Dad's party."

"Yes. When that snot-nosed Bradley called you an ugly duckling on the dance floor?"

"Yes. I… He rescued me. And I think in my head it became something. I hid it, deep down, but not far enough and when I needed help he was the one I thought of. I know that moment didn't make him…want me. But since then… We've been married, you know? I thought maybe he had some kind of attachment to me but I don't know if he has an attachment to anyone or anything."

"What about you?" Violet asked.

"What about me?"

"Do you feel something for him? I mean, more than your crush."

"Well… Who wouldn't?"

"A lot of people. He's quite difficult. That's why even though I also had a crush on him at one point I let it go a long time ago. I prefer men who are a little bit less...*hard.*"

"He is hard. But I think he's good. He had a hard life, but he wants to do the right thing, in spite of the fact that I don't think anyone has ever shown him what the right thing is. Well, anyone except Dad. But he's convinced that he's not... Really a part of our family."

"Well, he is now. By marriage at the very least."

"That might be the only thing he really likes about me."

"I don't think so."

Unspoken between them was the truth that if he really wanted that, he would have married Violet. Not just because she was more beautiful, but she was older. It made more sense. In just about every way.

"Well. It's an asset. He really only agreed to the marriage because he wanted to help me. And now... We're married. So he's making the most of it. At least from a business standpoint."

"And you love him?" Violet pressed.

"No," she said, the denial kicking hard

against her chest. "I'm not that silly. I'm not. I know that he's not ever going to feel that way about me. I think we can have a partnership, but I just have to figure it out…"

"You're not cut out for halfway, Minerva. That's your problem. You keep hiding yourself because you're afraid that you can't measure up to Maximus and me, but nobody ever asked you to. I'm not like Maximus. It would be easy for me to say that what I do is superficial. He bails people out of pretty terrible situations. And I'm sure that he would tell you sometimes he feels guilty about the people that he rehabilitates images for, since they oftentimes don't deserve it. But we do what we do, and we are who we are. Whoever you're destined to be… That's you. And you were never meant to live in shadows or to be quiet. And that's why you just… Shrink in on yourself altogether. Because if you speak out, you know it's going to be loud. And if you love, you know it's going to be big. That's good. It's not a bad thing."

Sure, it was easy for Violet to say. Minerva

would be the one left with a fatally broken heart.

"You should wear the red dress," Violet said.

"Red?" Minerva questioned. "But I'll be so... Conspicuous."

"Be conspicuous, Min. You've been hiding in books, in the garden, behind that horrible mean-kid stuff that happened to you in high school. They don't get to decide who you are, you do. Isn't it time that you took center stage?"

"I have done that multiple times over the last few weeks," Minerva pointed out. "First of all at your product launch. Second of all at the engagement party, then at the wedding..."

"And you did it for Isabella. Do something for yourself. Is that so wrong?"

"Yes," Minerva said. "Because I'm not... I'm just me."

"Yes, you're just you. And you is pretty amazing. Be kinder to her."

"I am being kind to her. I'm hiding away from the potential broken heart."

"No. You're hiding away from life. You let

all that stuff get in your head. You let yourself think that you were less than we are."

"I'm not as pretty."

"That's a lie. It's all about how you present yourself. And there's nothing wrong with being you. There's nothing wrong with not being flashy. I can't be anything else. I have to wander around with a pound of my product on my face all the time."

"I would look silly that way."

"Yes. You would. Not because you aren't beautiful, but because it isn't you. Different is fine. Different is good. But don't accept less."

"So what should I do? Put on the red dress and demand that he love me?" The very idea made her skin crawl.

She'd cared about a boy once, and she'd thought he'd cared too. Instead he'd humiliated her on a dance floor.

"Yes. Have you ever considered demanding that he love you? Because it might not be the worst thing in the world."

"Or it might be," Minerva said darkly.

"Or it might not be."

"I don't even know if I love him." But she was beginning to accept that that was a lie.

"Then I guess the question is… Are you going to stay with him even if you don't love him?" Violet asked.

"He can be Isabella's father…"

"So what? Set her aside for a second. Or, don't even set her aside. Would it be good for her to watch you live with someone you're miserable with? And who cares about Dad and Dante and their business thing? They can work that out on their own. It's not up to you, Minerva. If you love him, then you should demand more. If you don't love him, then you should demand more too."

"When did you become an expert on love?"

"I'm not." Violet's denial was vehement. "This isn't about knowing anything about love. But I do know a little bit about life. I know that if you are successful people are going to come after you, and it's easy to get caught up in trying to please everyone. No matter how independent and strong someone seems. You're caught up in this idea that you're not special, and I think because of that you work too hard to please everyone around you. And you don't work hard enough at pleasing yourself."

"The red dress?"

"Whatever makes you happy. Not what you think will make him happy, or even me happy. And not what you think you should wear. What do you want to wear?"

She got off the phone with her sister and she looked at the dresses again.

The red one.

She really did want to wear the red one. And why wasn't she wearing it? Because a boy had embarrassed her four years ago? Because she'd let the kids at school make her feel like she was ugly, like her family was the only interesting thing about her?

Because she'd chosen to get lost in the quiet nooks and crannies of her home when she was a child, lived in books, lived in her head, and then wondered why she felt left behind sometimes?

She wasn't like everyone else. But did that mean there was something wrong with her? Or did it just mean she was her?

Slowly, and with great care, she took the dress out of the bag and took it off the hanger.

She slid the glorious fabric over her body. It was slinky and perfect, molding to the curves that she had, making the most of her figure.

She worked on her hair, and her makeup, employing tips from videos that Violet had posted online.

She didn't do them quite like Violet. She did them like herself. And when she was finished, she felt...beautiful.

She felt like she was stepping out into the spotlight. Into something new and frightening. And she didn't know why it should seem that way. Because it wasn't as if any of this centered on her. Not really.

Except it felt like it did.

When she emerged in the living room, Dante was standing there looking beautiful in a suit, a crisp white shirt and a black jacket that conformed perfectly to his masculine physique. His dark eyes were unreadable, and passive as they took her in. "Are you ready?"

Her kneejerk response was to ask if she

looked ready. To ask him why that was even a question. If there was something wrong with what she had chosen. But she knew that she looked amazing, and she didn't need to be insecure. She didn't need to question anything.

She lifted her head and squared her shoulders. "Yes," she said. "I'm ready."

CHAPTER THIRTEEN

DANTE COULDN'T KEEP his eyes off Minerva. She was stunning in red. Her lips were the same crimson color to match, her eyeliner dark and winged. Her green eyes seemed like emeralds tonight. Had he ever thought that she was anything less than stunning? Had he ever thought that she was somehow the less beautiful King?

He couldn't even think of her as one of them, not now. She was set apart.

Glorious and otherworldly, because it all seemed transcendent of here and now. It wasn't just beauty for the eyes. He could breathe it in. Taste it. Feel it settle over his bones.

And yet, there was something about this beauty that felt like a challenge. It made him hesitant to touch her, and Dante was never hesitant.

But when they got out of the limo in front of the museum where the gala was being held, he pressed his hand against her lower back, a show of possession before the two of them walked up the stairs and made their way into the venue.

He didn't need to check in at the door, because everyone recognized him by face alone. At first, he thought Minerva might shrink against his side, but instead she stood proud. And when he introduced her as his wife, the mother of his child, she smiled and shook hands with each person with extreme confidence.

He didn't know what had possessed her this evening, but it was doing a very fine job.

After a time, music began to play and the guests filtered out onto a dance floor. Minerva saw this, and her eyes went wide, then she blinked rapidly. He knew just what she was thinking of.

That night four years ago.

He had seen the whole thing. And he had lied to her when he'd said that her father put him up to anything.

He had watched that boy take her out onto the dance floor, lean in and whisper something in her ear. And then he had watched as she crumpled.

And he had taken pictures. Wrapped his arm around her shoulder, taken a selfie with a tear-streaked Minerva and himself.

And that was when Dante had stepped in.

"I have been waiting to dance with you all evening, Ms. King."

And though he knew Minerva hadn't seen it, the boy had paled. And he had looked… Perhaps like he thought he had made a grave mistake.

She had felt slight and bony to him as he held her. Her body had changed quite a bit since then.

He had felt… Protective of her at that time. Like when he had helped her up off the ground when she had been much younger, her knee skinned.

He had always wanted to protect Minerva.

And now she had come into his sphere as his wife, and the fact of the matter was there was no way for him to protect her from himself.

But they were here.

And she was beautiful.

So they might as well dance.

"Would you like to dance with me? And no, before you ask, I have no designs to humiliate you."

A small smile touched her lips. "Okay. If you really want to."

He smiled in return, because he couldn't help himself, and he took her out to the center of the dance floor, holding her close and spinning her. Then he drew her back to his chest. She looked up at him, the smile on her face brilliant.

It was a strange thing, to be with Minerva apart from the baby. Without her present as a clear and obvious reason why the two of them were together. Yes, they had spent time alone together, but it had all been in service of Isabella.

It had nothing to do with a farce. There was no reason for a farce anymore.

He could let them go. They would be safe.

For some reason, the idea filled him with

a hollow kind of terror, and he couldn't account for why.

He drew her close, leaned in and whispered in her ear. "What did he say to you? That night at your father's party."

Her eyes went misty. "Do we have to talk about that?"

It still bothered her. It was hard for him to imagine that. He'd lived through poverty. Loss and pain. And it wasn't so much that he didn't think people like her—people who lived in comfort and relative ease—didn't also feel pain for the things in their lives. It was simply that of all the things he'd ever cared about, the good opinion of others wasn't often one of them.

Robert, he cared about his opinion because the man had changed his life.

But in general, he'd never... He'd been thrust into private school with boys who had been privileged and cosseted all their lives. They'd either found Dante to be a source of fascination, or something quite beneath them.

He hadn't care for either. But he hadn't cared about it, either.

He'd had trouble connecting. The only person who had ever mattered to him was Maximus. Their friendship had been unsteady at first, Maximus clearly not understanding why his father had ever cared much about the Roman urchin he'd pulled off the streets.

Eventually, slowly, rooming together at boarding school had brought them closer together. Dante had told Maximus about holding his father at gunpoint and he knew then it would either break their bond or solidify it forever.

Maximus had nodded and said: "You do what you have to, I guess."

And so, solidified their bond had been.

Whatever anyone else thought hadn't mattered. Minerva, though, was still clearly haunted by her humiliation.

Witnessing that had enraged him, and it bothered him she was still hurt.

That no man had stepped in to heal that wound.

You're her husband. The only one she'll have.

It was a profoundly depressing realization.

For *her.*

Another man might have eased this pain already, but he had not. Suddenly he found that he did want it. More than anything.

"I want to know," he said.

"He... He just said that I was stupid if I thought he really wanted to be here with me. He just wanted to be at the party. Wanted to see the house. Being my date was a dare. What he really wanted was a chance to see my sister."

"I see," Dante said. "What is more beautiful? A ruby or an emerald?"

"I don't understand."

"What's more beautiful, a tropical island or a desolate mountain?"

"They're both beautiful," she said. "Just different."

He nodded slowly. "Exactly. There are some things you cannot compare, Minerva, because they are not alike. One is not less. You cannot compare yourself to Violet. She's beautiful. She's successful. I don't want her. I do want you," he said, his voice rough. "Because the truth of the matter is, whether an emerald or ruby are equal in beauty, or a tropical island or a mountaintop are both perfect in their natural splendor, there is always one that a man prefers. And it has nothing to do with how it looks, not really. But what calls to his soul. And in this case, to my body. That's you. I cannot explain it. But it is."

"You don't sound very happy about it."

"I'm not. I was very happy to go through my life never having been bewitched, Minerva, and finding myself held in thrall by a woman that I have known for more than half my life is a very strange thing. I am not sure how it happened. This is not the first time we danced, but it is not the same as that first time."

"But still, when the pictures get published in the paper I imagine the headlines will be the same."

"I don't think so," he said. "But even then, what do you believe about yourself? What you know to be true, or what a bunch of strangers say about you?"

"I don't know," she said. "But… I do like what you said about me. I suppose, even if I can't win with strangers, I can content myself to have nice things said by you. Does this mean that we are going to be… Nicer to each other again?"

"I hope I was never unkind to you."

"I felt lonely."

"I don't know how to be a husband," he said.

"You were doing a pretty good job a minute ago."

"The last thing I want in this world is to hurt you, Minerva. I have done my best to protect you when I could. I owe a great debt to your father for all that he did for me. I would never want to harm what was most precious to him."

"Is that the only reason you don't want to hurt me?"

"No," he confirmed. "But that doesn't mean I won't. You have to be careful with men like me."

"You keep saying that. But the man that you are for the rest of the world… He's not the man that I've seen."

"You have such faith in me, Min, and I fear it is misplaced."

"I don't think so," she said, smoothing her hand up his chest.

His body reacted. Violently.

He pushed her back, the motion reflexive. Like he'd been burned.

"Sorry," he said. "I see David Carmichael back there." Thankfully, that was true. "Your father wished for me to speak with him before we leave."

"Oh…okay."

He took her hand and led her from the dance floor and was summarily stopped by a floppy-haired blond man in a suit that looked intentionally askew. It took him a moment, but he recognized him.

Chad Rothschild. A spoiled asshole he knew from his years in boarding school. Someone who had been friends with Maximus until Dante. Then he'd made an ass of himself pretty routinely all the years since.

"Dante," he said. "What a surprise to see you here."

To see he wasn't back in the gutter, Dante

imagined. Though Chad had to know he was not, as his reputation was legend. Chad's, on the other hand, consisted of many instances where he'd had to say, *But my father's a lawyer*.

"I don't see why it should be," Dante said. "This is, after all, where I do business. I am not sure what it is you do."

"Investments." A code for nothing. Chad's eyes flickered over Minerva. "Well, your ugly duckling certainly cleans up well."

"Excuse me?" Dante asked.

He felt Minerva begin to tremble then. "I'm teasing. But surely you've seen that old picture of the two of you. I have to hand it to you, you seemed quite chummy with Maximus in school. I had no idea you were messing with his sister."

Dante's lip curled. "I was not."

"If I were going to do that it would have been the other one."

"I'm sorry," Dante said. "Am I having a stroke? Are we back in boarding school?"

Chad kept on as if he hadn't heard the warning buried in each of the words Dante had just spoken. "She's not exactly the fabled beauty of the King clan, but I suppose if you have access to Robert King's millions and influence you're going to take what you can get. Though I thought that your own wealth exceeded that."

"My wealth is not in question. Neither is the beauty of my wife. I think it's apparent to all here that she is the most beautiful woman in the room."

"Undoubtedly, she is compelling," Chad said. "But I'm surprised you didn't marry her sister instead."

Dante saw red. And not just the red of Minerva's dress. A red haze of rage covered his vision. But Minerva's gentle hand on his arm stopped him.

"I appreciate that money is the only reason you can think that someone might marry you," Minerva said. "But that isn't the way it is for everyone. I care about Dante. We have a child together. I care about him more than anyone will likely care for you unless you do something to fix your repellent personality. Undoubtedly, someone will marry you for your money. But if I were you I would aim for more. It's quite sad."

And with her head held high, Minerva released her hold on Dante, and began to walk away. Dante went after her.

"What he said…"

"It's what people think," Minerva said.

"It doesn't matter what anyone thinks."

"No," she said. "It doesn't. Not really. It matters what I think. And the problem is that I believed the same thing for far too long."

He grabbed her arm and dragged her into a courtyard, away from the crowd. Away from prying eyes. And then he pinned her against the wall, his hand on her neck. "You incite me to madness," he growled. "No one else ever has. What he said… There is no reason for it. And he is wrong."

She touched his face. "But you didn't choose to marry me."

"Does that matter?"

"It always will to some people."

He arched his hips forward, letting her feel the effect that she had on him. "Does this feel like a choice to you?"

"No," she said. "I think even that you feel somewhat angrily."

He released his hold on her. Because she wasn't wrong. He hadn't chosen to feel what he did for her. It rearranged things inside him, and he didn't like it. He couldn't find where he had put his resolve, his reserve. He couldn't find himself at all. And he found it nearly unbearable. But it was no more unbearable than spending nights in separate rooms.

That he could truly no longer endure.

"We should leave," Dante said.

"Don't you have a business deal to make?"

"I will make it later. And I will make it without using you as a pawn. I will not subject you to more censure and speculation."

"Dante…"

"Your father will understand. And if he doesn't… Well. That's hardly my problem."

He had to get out of here. Before he did something they would both regret. Either to Chad or to her.

He felt… At the end of himself. And he

didn't know what Minerva had done to him to make him feel this way.

He had no way to correct course, because he couldn't understand where the wrong turn had come. Heart pounding, he grabbed her hand and made his way toward the exit. He sent his driver a text, and the limo met them outside.

"Drive around the block until I tell you to stop," Dante said.

When they tumbled into the back of the cab, he grabbed her, kissing her, hard and deep, pouring all of his anger, his frustration and confusion into the kiss.

He didn't do fear.

He didn't do confusion. He was above it. Beyond it. He had ascended in life, and he refused to be dragged back there. Certainly not at the delicate hands of Minerva.

He didn't need anyone.

He didn't need anything. He had learned long ago that he had to depend only on himself to survive. That he could not expect anything from anyone. Simply because he had received kindness from Robert King didn't mean that he could come to expect it from anyone else.

He didn't even take it for granted from Robert.

And then there was Minerva. For whom everything was so simple. Isabella had needed her, and so she had made herself available.

She claimed that she knew she didn't want another man, ever, in spite of the fact that she had no other experience of sex, and couldn't possibly understand what she might truly want in a few years.

No, for her everything was so straightforward. So simple.

And he wanted to…punish her for that. Something in him did.

So he kissed her. And it wasn't a kind kiss. Wasn't a nice kiss. Wasn't infused with the kind of gentleness that he had tried to inject into all the lovemaking on the island after he had discovered that she'd been a virgin their first time together.

Her dress was exquisite, beautiful. Off the shoulder and clinging to her curves just so.

He tore it down, revealing her breasts, their gorgeous, rosy tips, to his inspection.

She was perfection, was Minerva, and that man who had dared to make commentary on her beauty deserved no thought from her.

Even in his anger, anger that was unwieldy and reserved for any target in his path right now, he could not deny her beauty.

Her beauty was the only thing that made sense.

Because nothing else did.

Nothing else felt like him.

On the heels of that thought came another one, far more disturbing.

That he wasn't sure exactly what him was.

A boy who had tried to throw a birthday party for his mother. A boy who had found her dead the next morning of an overdose and had held her body and cried for hours. Afraid to leave her. Afraid that if he didn't no one would ever come.

The boy who had held the gun to Robert King's head.

The one who had taken his education and transformed it into a billion-dollar industry.

The one who was here now in the back of the limousine with Minerva, kissing her as though she were oxygen and he would die without her.

None of it felt real.

Except her hands. Her mouth. The physical sensation of touching her, holding her.

That was real.

He wondered which piece of her was real.

The little girl who had run around on the estate and fallen out of trees, skinning her knees and terrifying her mother.

The dreamy teenager with her nose stuck in a book.

The brave tigress who had demanded marriage to protect her cub.

The woman in his arms now.

Were they all every piece of those things?

And how did they bring them together?

Was it even wise to do so?

All those questions burned away in his consciousness as Minerva kissed him back. As her hands went to his tie, loosening it and undoing the buttons there. He batted those hands away.

He leaned down, taking one pert nipple between his lips and sucking it in deep.

She gasped, arching against him. But she wouldn't hold still, and her hands were skimming over him. He grabbed hold of her arms and pinned them to her sides, holding her still as he continued to lavish attention on her breasts.

He had to have the control here. She couldn't.

"Dante… Your driver can't…"

"Soundproof," he said.

"You told him to drive until you asked him not to."

"Undoubtedly he knows," Dante said. "But why should I be ashamed? Why should I be ashamed that I can't keep my hands off you? That I need to have you now. That I cannot wait until we are safely ensconced in the penthouse."

He was asking himself that question as much as he was asking her.

"Why should I be ashamed of you?" he said, their eyes meeting. He pulled her dress down as far as he could, until he met resistance at her hips. Then he moved down her body, grabbing hold of the hem of her skirt and pushing it upward. He exposed her legs, grabbed the center of her panties and swept them aside, exposing the heart of her. "How could I ever be ashamed of you?"

He pressed his fingers down against her, spreading her wide, then leaning in to taste her. Deep and lavish and long.

She tasted like Minerva. Amazing how distinct that had become to him. Unmistakable. This woman.

This woman.

One who had known more versions of him than any other woman he had ever taken as a lover.

But she was more than a lover.

More than his friend's sister, that was for damn sure.

She was his *wife*.

He growled, his ministrations on her body intensifying, surging forward, his hands joining in with his mouth as he pleasured her. As he pushed her to new heights. As he kept at her until she cried out. Until she pulsed with pleasure, her orgasm crashing over her, causing her to shake and shudder out his name.

After that, he couldn't wait anymore. Couldn't wait to join himself to her. He needed her. And he didn't want to admit to need. It was anathema to him. This feeling in his chest. The sense that he no longer belonged to himself.

That somewhere along the line he had lost some of himself in her.

But he couldn't stop himself either.

No. All he could do was take control.

"Up here, sweetheart," he said, lifting her and then turning her so that she was facing away from him, her face to the window, to the cars that were passing them by.

"Dante…"

"No one can see," he said. "The windows are tinted."

"Oh," she said. And he wondered if that was what she was even asking him about. Or if there was something about this that bothered her.

It wasn't up to her.

"I'm going to take you like this," he said, his voice rough.

He undid the closure on his pants and freed himself, pressing the blunt head of his arousal to the entrance of her body. Sliding into her was like coming home. She was perfect. In this, they were perfect. This was right, it was good. Because she needed him. This wasn't simply his wild need. No, she was right there with him. And that made him feel powerful. That reminded him that he was the one in control. Not her.

He plunged into her, and she gasped, arching against him. And he gripped her hips, slamming her back against him. She whimpered, her face pressed against the window.

"Dante," she whispered.

Over and over she said his name as he drove himself home. Until she was sobbing his name. Until she couldn't control herself at all.

Until he felt like he had fixed some of what had gone wrong inside him.

He knew this. And he knew who he was.

This was only sex. That was all.

She was beautiful, so of course she appealed to him. But that was all. It was all.

He repeated that himself, over and over again. She might have been any beautiful woman.

But then she looked back over her shoulder and the light from the neon that flashed on the buildings outside illuminated her face. Those green eyes.

And he knew it could only be her. Minerva.

She began to shake. Her climax taking her over.

"Dante," she said, whispering his name one more time.

He clenched his teeth shut to keep from saying hers.

But his orgasm consumed him, grabbed him by the throat and shook him.

Minerva.

Her name echoed inside him, but he refused to give it voice. He refused. But the deep, physical need came for him all the same, and he was spent, destroyed in the aftermath of his release. Splintered.

Except he was coming to realize that the splinter wasn't new.

Something had broken in him indefinably when he was young. And he had no earthly idea what could be done about it. He had the feeling that the answer was contained somewhere in her. He rejected that. And he pulled away.

He was Dante Fiori. And whatever he wanted, he could have. Whatever he needed was contained inside himself. He did not need anyone else. Least of all his friend's little sister.

He straightened in the limo. "Fix your clothes," he said.

She looked at him with wide eyes, but she complied. Then he lowered the window between himself and the driver. "You can take us home now."

He felt very much like he had broken something. But he could not quite put his finger on what.

And he could not give a reason for why it bothered him at all.

CHAPTER FOURTEEN

MINERVA HAD TAKEN herself to her bed and cried herself to sleep after she and Dante had gotten home.

She hadn't wanted him to be quite so careful with her sexually as he had begun to be, but she hadn't wanted that either.

It had been physically wonderful. It had left her feeling emotionally hollow.

He had used that position to distance her from him. And when she had looked behind her and established a connection with him, he had been very apparently angry.

She wrapped her arms around herself and looked out at Central Park. It was so cold outside.

She didn't actually know if it was cold. She hadn't checked. She hadn't been outside and she hadn't looked at anything to see what the temperature actually was.

But she assumed that it was. Because of all that gray.

Maybe the gray was inside her. Because if she stopped staring at it all like one big chunk, she could see the grass, she could see the trees.

But somehow, she couldn't feel them.

She was upset. And she supposed she didn't have anyone to blame but herself.

Last night had been a perfect opportunity for her to tell Dante how she felt.

After all, she hadn't hesitated to tell Chad how she felt.

But then, even though she had stood up for herself in the moment, she had also felt small when he had said those things. Because they echoed inside her.

Because they played at certain insecurities that she had no matter that she had put on a red dress. When it came to mothering Isabella, her confidence had grown.

When it came to other areas of herself… She was still a work in progress.

She sighed heavily, and went to check on Isabella, who was kicking happily in her crib.

She picked her up, and set her in a swing out in the living room so she could gaze out at the park too.

She had a feeling that Isabella didn't particularly care.

She should be happier. There was no threat on Isabella's life. The paperwork for the adoption was very nearly finished. Everything was easier because of Dante's money.

Her father had money, so it wasn't as though she didn't know that things were easier when you had it. It was just that Dante wielded his with authority and power, and even when it came to the workings of the upper class, Dante seemed to command a greater amount of attention than those around him.

He was one of those men. Legendary. Whispered about in every room he entered.

And she had been around him all her life.

He had a great impact on her, even with all that familiarity.

She almost felt sorry for women who hadn't had such long exposure to him.

He was devastating even with it.

Of course, it was more than just physical

devastation that she experienced when she looked at him.

She was in the grips of soul-deep devastation. She had no idea what to do with it.

She sighed heavily and turned to the laptop that was sitting on the marble island that separated the kitchen from the living room. She pulled up a homepage, and much to her surprise saw her face staring back at her from the society pages.

She had a triumphant smirk on her face, and she was standing in front of Dante, who was left slightly blurred.

Fiori's New Wife Unleashes Fury at Gala

She read on, and saw that the article described in great detail the way that she had flayed that ridiculous man the night before. The article concluded that she had been wrongly overlooked all this time, because she was clearly much more interesting than anyone had given her credit for.

She stared at the woman there in that picture. She looked strong. She looked confident.

Her phone buzzed and she looked down at it.

You wore the red.

Her sister Violet's text of triumph made something resonate in her chest.

She had.

And she had come out on top.

Except…

Still not with Dante.

Well. She was the only person that could fix that.

Minerva King had allowed herself to be leased for far too long.

It was finally time for her to do something for herself.

She made sure that Isabella was taken care of for the evening by her nanny, and she prepared dinner. Now all she had to do was wait for him to come home. She really hoped that he did.

It wasn't like he had ever not come home, but he sometimes did come home late.

She could have texted him, but she didn't want to.

Because she didn't want to...

Oh, there was no point trying to play it cool.

She had never done it, not once in her life. There was no point starting now.

She picked her phone up.

I made you dinner.

She waited. And waited for a response. Five interminable minutes went by without a response.

You didn't have to do that.

Obviously. Since I don't normally.

I'll be a little while yet.

Come home soon.

I have to finish some things.

Come home now.

She didn't get a response after that, and she paced around waiting.

Ten minutes later, the door to the penthouse opened. "I don't take orders."

She smiled and smoothed her hands over the tight, emerald green dress she was wearing. "Except, clearly you do take orders. Because here you are."

"A coincidence. I managed to finish everything on time. Why did you make dinner?"

"Because I wanted to… On our wedding night we didn't have dinner together. And I would like to have dinner together. It's different now that we're here. We are making a home together. The island was… Something else. It was removed from this. From reality. And here we are. Here we are together. This is our life. Isabella is going to legally be our daughter soon. Dante, I'm happy."

He raised his dark brows. "I'm glad."

"Are you?"

He lifted a shoulder. "I am as I ever am."

"What does that mean?"

"What did you fix?"

She noted he didn't answer, but she went ahead and let him redirect.

"Steak," she said. She waved her hand toward the table.

He cast a glance at it. "Let's eat."

They went over to the table, and Minerva scampered after him, moving to sit across from him. He was being as opaque and maddening as he'd been the night before.

They started to eat in silence. Minerva was feeling frustrated. But, she wasn't going to say anything. She had a feeling that he was doing all of this by design, she just couldn't work out why.

He seemed to enjoy dinner, and when it was done, she served dessert.

Chocolate lava cake.

She held it out to him, and her heart was pounding. It reminded her of that night on the island. When he had offered cake to her. When she had realized that more than the dessert was a temptation when it came to Dante. He didn't seem to remember that. Didn't seem to get the reference that was happening here at all.

Well. She could fix that.

She stood from her seat and unzipped her

dress, letting the top fall down, then letting the rest of it fall along with it. Then she walked over to where he was sitting, completely naked except for her high heels.

"There is a second offering for dessert."

He looked up at her, and he pushed the cake into the center of the table. "I think I'll have that now," he said.

"Not yet," she said.

She leaned forward and unbuttoned his shirt, pushing it down his shoulders. He stood, and she began to work at the belt on his pants, pushing them down his legs. And then, she sank to her knees before him.

"Minerva," he said, his voice rough.

But she ignored the warning in his tone. Ignored it completely as she leaned forward and let her tongue dart out, tasting him. Taking him into her mouth.

He groaned, fisting her hair in his hand, holding her steady as she began to pleasure him.

Her position was submissive, to be sure, but he was the one who was shaking beneath her attentions.

It was exhilarating. Doing to him what he'd done to her so many times. But she hadn't been brave enough to do this. Not before. Not because she didn't think she would like it but because she was afraid he would compare with other women and find her wanting. But she finally understood.

Experience didn't matter. Because no other woman could bring to the table what she did, here and now. It was their connection. And that was why he was afraid.

He was pulling away from her because everything in the two of them was drawing them to each other. There was no denying it. There was no escaping it. No matter what he thought. She curved her hand around his shaft, stroking him in time as she continued to pleasure him with her mouth.

"Minerva," he growled. "Enough." She did not obey. But then, he pulled on her hair, and she had no choice but to go with him.

She was suddenly embarrassed, because what they'd done was in a public part of the house, and while the nanny had been given instructions to stay in the nursery, there was still the possibility they could have been walked in on. Except… They hadn't been. And she found it very difficult to care one way or another.

Dante picked her up, and began to carry her from the room, shucking the rest of his clothing as he went. The trail of clothes would be a clue if nothing else. But again, she couldn't find it in her to care.

He took her into his bedroom, the first time she had been there since they had returned from the island. And he set her in the middle of it, spreading her across the bedspread.

She parted her thighs for him, touching herself as she watched him, looked at his body while he stood there. At his proud masculinity, at the well-defined muscles.

"You're beautiful," she said.

She had nothing to hide. She felt free.

Joyful.

This was sex as it was meant to be. The exchange was more than just bodies. So much more.

He came down on the mattress with her,

thrusting inside her body, and she gripped his shoulders.

"I love you," she whispered.

He growled, pulling out and slamming back home. "I love you," she said again, in case he hadn't heard her the first time.

He had heard.

But he was doing his best not to respond, she could tell.

So she said it. Over and over again until it blurred with whimpers of pleasure. Until she lost herself in it. In him.

Until she was certain that the feelings had come straight from her chest and wound themselves around the two of them, that it had joined in with the physical sensation. That it was a real and living entity in the room with them.

Love.

She loved him.

And she wanted him to love her back.

Wanted it, deserved it. Needed it.

If she wasn't ashamed. No. She wasn't ashamed.

And she didn't feel undeserving. She didn't. She deserved it all. Everything.

He flexed against her, his body hitting that sensitive bundle of nerves between her legs, and she cried out, pleasure breaking over her like a wave.

Love echoing in her like a storm.

"I love you," she said, one last time before he shook and shuttered and gave himself over to his release.

And when he pulled away, she knew what he was doing.

She knew already that he was going to try to run from this like he had tried to run before.

But he had been able to get as far as he had only because she hadn't challenged him. But she was going to challenge him now. Yes, she was. She was going to challenge him and she was going to demand what she wanted. Was going to demand everything she deserved.

"I love you," she said again.

"I don't know what you expect me to say to that."

"Well, I would like for you to say that you love me too."

"I can't," he said.

"Can't or won't?"

"It amounts to the same thing in this instance."

"No. It doesn't. Dante, I know that your childhood was difficult. I know that your mother hurt you. But this is different. We are a family. We can be different."

"No," he said, turning away from her. "That's enough, Minerva. I will care for you, I will take care of you and I will be faithful to you, but asking anything more of me is unnecessary."

"No," Minerva said. "It is not unnecessary. It is absolutely and utterly necessary. Because I have spent my entire life asking nothing. Nothing of myself. Nothing of anyone else. I have never demanded that I get everything because I thought for some reason I didn't deserve it. I always felt like the small sparrow in a family filled with glorious peacocks. And I sank down into that role because I was afraid that if I wanted anything more I would be in pain for all of my life. I was afraid that if I asked for something more it would confirm what I believe secretly. That I couldn't have it. That for some reason I wasn't put together in such a way that I deserved it. But I know better now. I want this life, not just for Isabella, but for me. I want love because I deserve it. And so do you. We don't deserve anything less than everything, Dante, and there's no reason we shouldn't have it."

"There is every reason," he said. "Love is a lie. Love is just waiting for other things to come in and prove themselves more powerful. You know what is more powerful than love? Fear. Addiction. Poverty. These things can destroy love. They can defeat it. Trust me, I've seen it. I have no desire to have it again."

"You see examples of love all around you. All around you. There's no reason you shouldn't accept it for yourself. You know that what you're saying is a lie. If all these things exist in the world, why wouldn't you cling to love?"

"I don't want it," he said, turning back around again, grabbing hold of her arms and staring down at her with his fierce dark eyes. "I don't want you. Don't you understand that?"

"You don't... You don't want me?"

"I tried to pull away from you politely over the last few days. But it's become very clear to me that you don't actually understand what's happening between us. I thought that we needed this marriage, but we don't. There is no reason for the two of us to stay together. No reason at all. I don't need your father's money and Carlo is dead."

"It wasn't about me..."

"No. This is over. I will allow the adoption to continue with you and Isabella. I will withdraw my name."

"You're going to abandon Isabella?"

"It is for the best," he said. "I am no kind of father, and she no longer needs my protection."

"What about you? Don't you think she could possibly need you?"

"No. Nobody needs me. I have money, and I have power, and I wield it well. I wielded it to save you, but now that is over. This is done. We are done."

She sat there, utterly and completely devastated. And he began to collect his clothes. "I'm going back to the office," he said.

"No… Dante…"

"I will arrange for you to go back to San Diego tomorrow."

"I don't want to go back. This is my home."

"No," he said, his voice ragged. "Your home is with your family. And I am not your family."

And with that, he turned and walked out of the room, leaving her there with her heart broken in pieces around her feet.

She had asked for everything. In return, she had lost the biggest, brightest thing she'd ever dared reach for.

And all she could do was curl up in the center of his bed and cry.

CHAPTER FIFTEEN

WHEN DANTE RETURNED from his trip into the office, he could hear a soft, plaintive voice. Wailing. He stood in the middle of the room, unsure of what to do.

His eyes were dry and his lungs felt bruised, and he didn't know how he was going to proceed.

With anything.

Minerva had said that she loved him, and there was something about that that had destroyed everything that he built, and told himself he'd built for the last two decades.

How? How had one small woman and a baby utterly and completely taken all that he believed about himself in the world and turned it upside down?

No one should have the power to do that to him, much less her.

And the baby was still crying. Where was she?

Where was Minerva?

Isabella was not his daughter. And she wouldn't be.

He was going to put a stop to the paperwork that would make her his. Because it was the right thing to do. There was no other alternative. She wouldn't want him for a father anyway, and he would be an utterly useless one at that.

He couldn't love.

He couldn't. The baby was crying, and still Minerva wouldn't come. Neither did the nanny. He didn't understand what was happening.

He could go and get her. Wake one of them, as it was three in the morning and it was likely that they were asleep.

But he shouldn't have to.

It was an infant. Surely, he could handle whatever ailed her.

He charged into the room, and he stopped. He gazed down at her little, helpless body in the center of the crib, and everything inside him froze. She was just so… Small. Help-less. And he was brought again back to his childhood.

To the fact that his parents had created him, his mother had given him life, and had just…

He took a step closer to the crib. Slowly, he bent down, taking the tiny form into his arms and holding her close against his chest. He could hear his own breathing, ragged and intense above the sound of the little girl's cry-ing.

He cradled the back of her downy head, and she rubbed her face against him.

"Are you hungry?"

Something about his voice made her star-tle, then still.

He didn't know how to make a bottle, but he damn sure could figure it out.

And in the kitchen with one arm, that was what he did, while he cradled her close.

He took her back into the nursery, and sat in the rocking chair, looking down at her as he fed her. And he had no idea how he had wound up here.

With an infant.

But she wouldn't be here. Not in his house. Not anymore. Because she and Minerva were leaving.

Something seized in his chest, and then he felt as if everything broke in half. Like a seismic shock had gone through his entire body. This child could destroy him.

As easily as Minerva could.

That became clear in the moment.

This weak, helpless thing held a power over him that he couldn't understand.

She opened her little mouth, one side of her lip lifting higher than the other, and a small growl escaped her tiny body.

His tiger cub.

He was held in thrall just then. He couldn't look away. Couldn't pull away at all.

What was this feeling?

And more important, why did his mother not feel it for him?

Because one thing he knew for sure, feeling this on one side was absolutely the worst fate that could ever befall a man.

Because it didn't matter that his mother had been so distant, it didn't matter that she had hit him for throwing her birthday party. It didn't matter that she had overdosed and died and left him.

He had loved her still.

And no amount of telling himself he shouldn't, no amount of mourning could bring her back. It was pain. Utter, gut-wrenching pain. The kind that you didn't recover from.

And he would be damned if he ever gave anyone that kind of power over him ever again.

He couldn't.

It would be a blessing. That this was done now. Because Isabella would never remember him.

And someday, Minerva would find a man who could give her everything she wanted.

Already that thought hurt too much.

He laid Isabella down in the crib, comforted by the fact that she would have no memory of ever having held him.

But as he walked out of the room, he could

still feel the impression of her tiny body cradled in his arms.

And he knew that he would never be able to forget.

CHAPTER SIXTEEN

THANKFULLY, DANTE WAS not around when Minerva, the nanny and Isabella grimly loaded themselves onto his private plane and charted a course for San Diego.

She tried to hold her head high when she arrived at her parents' house, but the minute that she saw her mother she crumpled completely.

Her mother ushered her to sit down, and held her, and didn't say anything.

The entire story poured out of Minerva, all of it. The truth.

"But she will legally be yours?" her mother asked. "Soon?"

"Yes," she said. "Dante had all the paperwork processing. It's all over. But it's been… A nightmare. And we did everything we could to protect her. Everything we thought was right. I'm sorry that I didn't tell you. But…"

"Of course you didn't feel like you could chance anyone knowing," she said.

"I didn't. And it isn't because I didn't trust you…"

"You're her mother," Elizabeth said. "And you would do anything to protect her. Of course you did this. Of course."

Minerva nodded miserably and watched her mother hold Isabella.

"But he broke your heart?" Elizabeth asked.

"Yes," Minerva said. "He broke my heart. I don't know what to do about it. I don't know how I'm going to survive."

"You just will," Elizabeth said. "You will because you have her to live for."

"I just want to sit down and give up."

"But you won't do that either. It's okay to want to do that, as long as you don't."

"I just… I think it would've been fine if I hadn't demanded that he loved me. But I did. I demanded it because I thought… Don't I deserve it? Don't I deserve to have somebody love me?"

"Of course you do," her mother said.

"I know that I'm not beautiful like Violet, or successful. That I'm not magnetic like Maximus, and I'm definitely not a billionaire."

"What does that have to do with anything?"

"I just… They are exceptional."

"Minerva, you are now and always have been exceptionally you. Right down to this whole harebrained situation with the baby. You are utterly and uniquely yourself. And no one has ever been able to convince you to be anything but that. You're strong. And you're stubborn."

"No I'm not. I always just kind of… Go along with things."

"If you think that, then you don't even know yourself all that well."

"Well. Maybe I don't."

"Look at yourself. You stole this baby. You protected her with your life. You roped Dante into everything in spite of the fact that he is a terrifying and powerful man to most everyone else. Very few people would have dared to do what you did."

"I had to."

"Then you married him. Then you demanded that he love you. Love is not less. It's brave. You're very brave. That isn't something that can be taught. I'm proud of you, Minerva. Not just for everything you did before, not just for what you did with Isabella, but for how you handled Dante."

Minerva felt broken and easily wounded, but she forced a smile, and allowed a moment of happiness in.

"It's going to be all right," Elizabeth said.

"But what if it isn't?"

"Because Dante is a smart man. And you are an exceptional woman. I don't think he's actually going to let you get away."

"And if he does?"

"Then he's not a smart man. But you are still an exceptional woman."

Minerva thought about that all through the rest of the evening and as she laid Isabella down to sleep.

Her mother was trying to help, and she knew that. But in the back of her mind she wondered if fairy tales were for other girls.

For the bright, the exceptional, the beautiful.

Then she looked down at Isabella.

No.

Of course that wasn't true. Of course it wasn't…

It took her breath away how obvious it seemed all of a sudden as she looked down at her own daughter.

What she deserved in life had nothing to do with looks. Or money. Success. It had nothing to do with what a boy at a dance said about her. Had nothing to do with whether or not the kids at school liked her or thought she was pretty.

She had value all on her own.

And so did Minerva.

Whether Dante ever realized it or not.

CHAPTER SEVENTEEN

"WHY IS MY sister back home?"

Dante looked up from his desk to see Maximus standing in his office doorway. No one should be standing in his office doorway. He paid his secretary well to keep that from happening. And Maximus really shouldn't be standing there.

"She missed her family," he said, keeping his expression neutral.

"Why is that?"

He pressed his hands on his desk and stood. "If you didn't know already that we're divorcing, then let me be the first to tell you. But I assume you did already."

"I didn't want to have to kill you, Dante, but I will."

"Maximus, I know you excelled in boxing at school, but I'm a street fighter. You're not going to kill me."

A dark glint shone in his friend's eyes and Dante had the sense that he had gone too far. "Your mistake is always underestimating me, friend. You don't know everything that I could do to you."

"Whether you believe it or not, Minerva was in control of all of this. And her leaving… I asked her to go to protect her."

"My mom told me the whole story. I know Isabella isn't your baby. I had a hard time believing it in the beginning, I have to admit."

"So, she told you what Minerva did?"

Maximus nodded. "And if my sister wasn't crushed, I wouldn't be here. I would assume that you had done what you did to protect her, and now the deal was done but obviously something happened between the two of you."

Dante lifted a shoulder. "I won't lie to you. She was my wife."

"What happened to your Catholicism?"

"Tell me," Dante said, his temper fraying, "what would be the greatest sin? To divorce your sister or keep her with me for the rest of my life. You know me, Maximus. You know that I'm not...part of your world, not part of the one I came from. Not part of Min's or Isabella's. You know that I don't know how to... I don't know how to be part of a family. Not even yours."

"Your own choice, Dante. We've always wanted you to be part of us."

"And I don't know how to do it," Dante said, frustration eating at him. "Tell me. How should I be a good husband to Min? You don't know how to be a husband. What can you tell me?"

"Nothing about that. Though I had thought that you were a decent human being. My father opened his home to you and I called you brother. Was I wrong to do that?"

Dante had told himself he didn't care about much. But hearing his friend ask him if he was wrong to call him brother made something crumble inside him. The bit of heart, of humanity, he had left.

"If you care about Minerva at all..." Maximus continued.

"I do," he bit out. "I love her."

The words made the back of his neck

prickle. Made sweat bead at his temples. He loved her. It was the thing he feared most because it was the one thing he could not control.

Not ever.

And he'd sworn he would never…

Minerva King.

She had been a girl when he'd first met her. How had she reached around inside him and changed him like this?

How had she become his dearest dream and greatest nightmare all at once?

"Then why are you doing this to the both of you? Go back to her."

His throat was dry. "I… I can't."

Maximus sighed heavily. "Please don't make me talk about feelings."

"*Dio.* Don't."

"You're forcing it. You're forcing me to."

"Can I stop you?"

"Quit being a jackass and go to my sister. Minerva is the kindest and most caring person I know. The kindest and most caring person I have ever known. If she loves you, you've done well for yourself, Dante."

"I never wanted to love another person again," he said.

"Well, what a tragedy. You found someone to love, who loves you very much in return. Some people would call that an unexpected gift. A lot like trying to rob a man at gunpoint only to get offered a chance at a new life. That was brave of you, to take that."

"Desperate," he said. "And I vowed I wouldn't be desperate again."

"Well, here you are I guess," Maximus said, looking around. "In all this glass and chrome. Not desperate at all. But meanwhile, across the country, there is a woman who loves you and a child who needs a father." He turned to go, then stopped. "And you know, the rest of us are fond of you too. My father reached out to you that day. Maybe it's time you reached back, brother."

And without another word, Maximus walked out of his office, as if he hadn't been there at all. And Dante was left with a burning sensation in his chest.

He loved her.

And she was not dead. She was not gone.

And he…he had pushed her away because he had no earthly idea what else to do other than…

Accept it.

The idea filled him with dread. The idea of loving her, loving Isabella.

He looked around his office. His glass and chrome. This tower, surrounded by that wall he'd built for himself.

His security.

And suddenly it all meant nothing.

Suddenly it was not a protection, but a barrier. A barrier between himself and Minerva. Brick after brick, built to keep him safe. Built to keep him separate.

It could not endure.

Not anymore.

He loved her.

And it was a gift to a heart that had given up on loving ever again.

But most of all, she might still love him.

Him, a man from nothing. A man who knew nothing of how to love except getting slapped in the face for it.

She had loved him first. Before he knew

how to show it or how to admit to himself that he loved her too.

But he couldn't stay safe. He couldn't stay on this side of the wall, not if he wanted her.

Suddenly it all seemed clear.

For love he would.

For Minerva, he had to. His girl, his *woman*. Who loved books and knew that his home had been patterned after *Swiss Family Robinson*. Who understood, somehow, these sharp, strange emotions inside himself that not even he understood.

He was done surviving.

He wanted to live.

CHAPTER EIGHTEEN

IT HAD BEEN a week of feeling like her heart was beating with ground glass inside it, painful and sharp. Minerva was tired of it. Tired of herself. But she was also resolved.

She'd started trying to figure out what she wanted from her life too.

With the help of some of Violet's business consultants she'd begun feeling out what it would take to start job training for single mothers, with special focus on those recovering from addiction, depression, or any woman trying to escape an abusive relationship.

The KatiBella Foundation was on its way to becoming a reality, and Minerva was happy to know that she could honor her friend's memory that way.

And that she could honor her daughter, her inspiration for the foundation in the first place.

But she was still…

She missed him. She loved him. She hated that she did.

She felt utterly, thoroughly grown up. She felt old, in fact. She couldn't believe that just a few months ago she'd come home with Isabella. That only a year ago she'd been in Rome, an innocent university student without a care in the world.

She felt like she had a world of care on her shoulders now.

But she wouldn't change it.

No.

She was…changed. She was in love. And she loved Isabella. She was heartbroken, but she was stronger somehow even in that brokenness. She couldn't explain it, but it was true.

Isabella was asleep, and Minerva hadn't had any luck sleeping at all lately. Instead of even trying, she stole down to the beach and looked out at the waves.

The moon reflected on the water, the sound reverberating around her.

And her heart went tight in her chest.

She missed him.

She wanted to see this with him. To be on the beach with him again. Kiss him again.

She knew what it meant to want someone now. To love them.

She also knew beyond a shadow of a doubt that she hadn't been heartbroken four years ago at her father's party. She'd been wounded, but not heartbroken.

This didn't feel like shame. There was pride mixed in with it. It didn't feel like sadness, because it felt more brittle. More aged. Like it had maybe always been inside her. This sense of what it was like to not have Dante.

She hated him for teaching her this.

But she loved him for teaching her so many other things. Even when he wasn't here.

She put her hand on her stomach and watched the waves crash into shore, the whitecaps visible even in the darkness. He might have given her more than a broken heart, and she really had no idea what she would do if her period didn't start in the next couple of days.

"You'll be okay," she whispered to herself.

Because she would be. She had become the heroine, over the course of these weeks, these months. And because of that, she knew everything would be all right in the end.

"Min."

The sound of her name rose up above the waves, and she turned, her heart stalling out completely when she saw him standing there. His face looked haggard in the moonlight. The hollows of his cheeks more pronounced, dark circles under his eyes that spoke of the same lack of sleep she had been experiencing.

"Dante."

For some reason, as Dante stood there on the beach staring at Minerva he felt more like that boy he'd been at fourteen, holding a gun he didn't want to use, his hands shaking, than he ever had in the intervening years since.

Perhaps it was because he was only standing there, with a heart pounding heavily in his chest that he didn't want to use.

But he had no choice.

After Maximus had come to see him, he had understood.

He had known beyond a shadow of a doubt that it was already too late to protect him. They had gotten under his skin, these two females who had moved into his home, his life.

Minerva, his tigress, and the tiger cub. Everything was upside down because of them.

Everything destroyed.

He had tried to make it right. He had gone back to work. He had tried to put another brick between himself and his past, but the problem was that the past had crashed through the wall and bled into his future.

It had made him turn Minerva away, and all he could think of was the incredible pain that had caused him. And then he thought he was going to have to build the wall again. In front of the time he spent with her. The nights making love. In front of those sun-drenched days on the private island.

In front of that night when he'd held Isabella in his arms and understood what it meant to be a father.

And he began to do that. Laying bricks. Over his heart, yet again. But he had realized that he didn't want to stop thinking about them, even if it hurt.

And so he was here. Because he didn't know where else to be.

"What are you doing here?"

"I'm here for you. I'm here to explain."

"It had better be a good explanation," she said, clenching and unclenching her hands into fists.

"I know," he said. "Minerva, it isn't that I don't believe in love. I do. But the problem is that I know what it's like to love someone who can't love you back. I know what it's like to be ill-used and abused and to not be able to let go. To want so badly for another person to care. She couldn't care. No matter how much I wanted my mother to care, she couldn't.

"And it broke me in ways that I can't begin to describe. Except to tell you that I was hollowed out by the time your father met me. I wanted to be ready to shoot him if I needed to get money, to get food. Instead, I found myself accepting his charity. And I thought to myself, *He's offering charity, he might well have disgraceful intentions for me*, and I thought that I could accept that too. I had lost my humanity somewhere in there. I… I lost my soul. Because I quit letting myself love.

"And even when I joined your family, it was the same. I told myself that I was different because I wasn't blood. I held Isabella the other night, and I knew blood had nothing to do with anything. It isn't because of him that I've been distant from your father. It's because of me. Because I never wanted to accept the gift that he offered me. This place in the family. Because I didn't want to need anyone or anything.

"I have been building walls ever since I escaped from Rome. Building walls between myself and the poverty that I had once. Because I thought they would keep me safe. Because I thought they would make it so I couldn't go back. But all they do is keep people out. People that you want. People that you need. And I can't live that way anymore. I can't. Because you showed me a better way. You showed me a better life.

"Minerva, I used to think of you as a mouse, but that isn't true at all. You're a tigress. You are brave and brilliant and you have taught me bravery. I'm sorry that I couldn't stand up and seize hold of it when I needed to. When you asked me to. But I want to do it now.

"Minerva, I am humbled by the gift that is you. You are the most brilliant woman who has ever been. Or ever will be. You are not second, you are first. It's only that my heart was blind. Because that's what it is when you take love away from yourself. You rob yourself of your senses. You make it so that you cannot truly see. But I see now. I see now because of you."

"Me?"

"Yes," he said. "You. You had to become a woman before I could have you, Min. And I... I should have waited until I became the man you deserved before I ever touched you."

"Dante," she said, flinging herself into his arms, wrapping them around his neck. And kissing him.

"That's it?" His voice was rough. "You're not even going to make me work for it?"

"We already worked for it. You already worked for it. And you know what? Even if you hadn't come to your senses, you taught me something. You taught me to demand everything."

"Good. Keep demanding it."

"I will. I will. Dante, you are the most brilliant man I have ever known. And I am really glad that I had to force you to marry me."

"I *want* to marry you again," he said.

"Really?"

"Yes. Not for spectators, not for show. I want to marry you again because I want to."

"Well. I'd like that."

"And then maybe this time your brother and father will want to kill me."

"Well…" she said. "They might."

"Why?"

She twisted her hands in front of her. "There is a small possibility that I might be a pregnant bride."

"What?"

"I'm late. And… We have been doing something that sometimes means…"

"Are you sure?"

"No. I'm not sure. If devastated broken hearts cause missed periods then that could be the problem. It's just that I think more likely it was pregnancy."

"But Isabella is only…"

"I know," she said.

"I'm going to be a father. Two children."

She laughed. "I know," she said. "Isn't that amazing?"

"I…"

His life flashed before his eyes. As if he was dying. Except he wasn't dying. He was living. And he saw himself, that boy in Rome with the shaking gun, angry and distrustful in private school, starting his first business endeavor, Minerva asking him to protect her. Him demanding she marry him.

All of it had brought him here. To this moment. There were no walls. And he was in no danger of going back. It was impossible. He had been afraid all this time that he might slip back into the slums by accident. But it had never been about the slums. They didn't matter at all. What mattered was this. The people in his life. And he would not lose that. He wouldn't lose them.

And he would never lose the love in his heart.

It had been said that Dante Fiori could condemn a man to any level of hell he chose with just the lift of his brow. That was a fabrication. But what was true was that Minerva King could send him to heaven with just the touch of her lips to his.

"I love you," he said.

"I love you too," she said.

And he knew that he would never be alone again.

He had a family.

Not tied together by blood, but by love.

And that was the most powerful force of all.

EPILOGUE

SHE WAS A pregnant bride. There was no denying that fact. But fortunately, they were technically already married.

Though, that did not stop her father from giving Dante an endless hard time. And it didn't stop her brother, Maximus, from giving him the evil eye, but then, Maximus hadn't stopped that at any point over the last few months.

Minerva wasn't put off by any of it. She was happy. The adoption for Isabella had gone through a couple of months earlier, and she and Dante were legally what they had already been in their hearts: her parents.

She was acting as their flower girl, even though Dante had to carry her down the aisle. And when the wedding was over, since the only guests were family and very close friends, when Minerva threw the bouquet, her sister, Violet, caught it, then stared at it like it was a live cockroach.

"Marriage might be coming for you," Minerva commented.

"Never," Violet said. "Though I like the colors in this bouquet. I could make a very nice makeup palette out of it. Use it as inspiration. I'll call it Minerva's Bouquet. The proceeds can go to KatiBella."

"That is the closest I will ever get to being a mogul," Minerva said.

"You could be one if you wanted to."

She put her hand on her stomach, and she looked at Dante, holding her daughter. "I'm everything that I want to be," she said.

"What's that?" Violet asked.

Minerva looked at her sister, her parents, her brother. Then again at her daughter and her husband.

"Loved."

And she was. For all her days.

* * * * *